GATES OF THE CITY

E|L

EMERGENT LITERATURES

Emergent Literatures is a series of international scope that makes available, in English, works of fiction that have been ignored or excluded because of their difference from established models of literature.

Gates

of

the

City

•

Elias

Khoury

University
of
Minnesota
Press

Minneapolis
London

Foreword
by
Sabah
Ghandour

Translated
by
Paula
Haydar

Published by the University of Minnesota Press
2037 University Avenue Southeast, Minneapolis, MN 55455-3092
Printed in the United States of America on acid-free paper

Library of Congress Cataloging-in-Publication Data

Khūrī, Ilyās,
　　[Abwāb al-madīnah, English]
　　Gates of the city / Elias Khoury : translated by Paula Haydar.
　　　　p.　cm. — (Emergent literatures)
　　ISBN 0-8166-2224-8 (alk. paper)
　　I. Title.　II. Series.
PJ7842.H823A6413　1993
892'.736—dc20　　　　　　　　　　　　　　　　92-32342
　　　　　　　　　　　　　　　　　　　　　　　　　　CIP

Contents

Foreword

Sabah Ghandour

The novel in Lebanon, as in the rest of the Arab world, is basically a new form that is said to be imported from the West.[1] Although the form itself is imported, the art of telling stories, as Marun `Abbud notes, is by no means a tradition acquired from the West.[2] The Arabs are known historically for their ability to tell and transmit stories. So we find "a rich assortment of narrative forms—*qissa, sira, hadith, khurafa, ustura, khabar, nadira, maqama*—"[3] all of which tell stories, but none of which has developed into a novel as we know it in the West and in the Arab world nowadays.[4]

Several studies have been written in Arabic and English discussing the historical development of the modern Arabic novel, whether in a specific country or as a whole.[5] These studies mainly examine the origin of the Arabic novel, following its development from the nineteenth century through the twentieth century into modern times. Some of these critical works interrogate the origins of the novel and its early development during the *Nahda,* "the movement of cultural revival or renaissance which began in earnest during the nineteenth century," and discuss the novel's achievement through its "period of maturity."[6] The development of the Arabic novel, then, has passed through different phases, from a period of translation and adaptation, through that of the educational novel dealing with historical or social issues, till it reached its modern phase, basically in the second half of the twentieth century.

The pioneers of Arab renaissance were primarily from Syria and Lebanon.[7] These renaissance pioneers, who immigrated to Egypt and to the Americas, translated innumerable books, mostly novels, from foreign languages into Arabic.[8] Whether the published works were translations, adaptations to an Arab environment, or purely constructed works of the imagination, their medium of communication was inevitably the Arabic language. This movement of translation in the *Nahda,* accompanied by the spread of journalism, helped simplify Arabic by making it more diversified and suitable to the times.[9] In fact, the debate between the traditionalist, who called for the preservation of the language intact and free from foreign influence, and the modernist, who advocated a reconsideration of tradition and the modification of classical Arabic language, had already started in the nineteenth century. Karam Milhem Karam, a pioneer of the modern Arabic Lebanese novel, criticizes a fellow translator, Tanyus `Abduh, for distorting the contents and mutilating the structure of the works he translated.[10] Karam criticizes `Abduh, however, mainly for his weak syntax and feeble vocabulary.[11] Karam is most interested in preserving the diction and structure of the classical Arabic.

This debate continued into the twentieth century and well into the present. Al-`Aqqad and al-Mazini, advocates of the traditional camp, called for the preservation of the classical Arabic idiom, while the Egyptian Salama Musa, and the two Lebanese Mikha'il Nu`aymah and Husayn Murruweh believed that language changes and develops over time, just as humanity progresses.[12] On one hand, al-`Aqqad vehemently opposes the employment of colloquial Arabic in literature. He emphasizes that " 'the spoken language of the mob' will never become the medium for literary creations of enduring value."[13] Moreover, al-`Aqqad criticizes Nu`aymah in his introduction of the latter's *al-Ghirbal* for employing some new vocabulary and expressions in his writings. Al-`Aqqad believes that Arabic should not change or develop, for it is an old language that has its own history and its own grammar, and whenever a language meets these conditions, there is no need to ignore them or to go against the prescribed rules.[14] On the other hand, Salama Musa advocated the use of colloquial instead of literary Arabic, for it is through using a simplified language that writers can reach a wider audience. He strongly believed that literary Arabic is "detrimental to the creation of national consciousness"[15] and that the " 'language of the people' would create a 'literature for the people,' with ideas relevant to their times."[16]

This debate over the use of language in the medium of literature started on a preliminary level but went far beyond the use of either idiom. It is a question that touches a sensitive issue in Arab history, that of Arab nationalism and identity. This debate has developed to encompass more sophisticated and complex issues as to what best represents the spirit of the nation and its identity. Language is traditionally regarded as the embodiment of the spirit of the age, by which I mean the concerns and aspirations, customs and traditions, and of course the dominant debates that take place at a certain time. Haykal, a contemporary of al-`Aqqad and al-Mazini's, believes the national writer is the one who best represents his or her age by gaining "recognition as an uncontested master of language. His neologisms will gain wide currency and acquire the place they deserve in all dictionaries."[17] Haykal, who in his early career advocated the use of the colloquial in the dialog for the sake of "verisimilitude," has reverted to a more conservative position in his later years. But, whatever his position, Haykal strongly believes in the "transparency" of the language. He makes a comparison between language and clothing to show that language is the shell or the cover for meaning, as clothes cover the body and convey the essence of individuals. As different fashions develop across time, so language develops to signify the changing object it represents.[18]

At the bottom of this battle between advocates of the old and the new, as it has been dubbed, there was a common denominator, namely, the contention that language reflects reality. Although it was "not accidental that left-wing writers favoured the use of the `ammiyya as a literary medium,"[19] it is also not the rule that such writers only favored the colloquial. For example, Muhammad Mandur, a left-wing critic, believes that literary Arabic "embodies our deep-rooted national culture. . . . *Al-Fusha* . . . is a solid foundation for Arab nationalism."[20]

This debate between the proponents of literary Arabic and colloquial Arabic engendered another debate between advocates of "life for literature" and "literature for life." In other words, it was a debate between those who favored art for art's sake and those who preferred committed literature. Taha Husayn believed in the autonomy of art because "literature is an end in itself."[21] He accused two progressive critics, Amin Mahmud al-`Alim and `Abdul `Azim 'Anis, of "calling for the burning of books and demolishing the pyramids in their efforts to eradicate tradition because they called the writers to be committed to the problems of their times."[22]

This controversy reached its peak in the 1950s, a decade that witnessed the 1952 revolution and 1956 war in Egypt, and the 1958 civil war in Lebanon. While some writers were calling for a socialist-realist literature that would speak directly to the people expressing their concerns in Egypt and elsewhere, "Sartre was the special favorite of Beirut's literary workshop."[23] Despite Sartre's emphasis on the self and the nature of the individual, he was steeped in practical politics, and his philosophy bears the imprint of his political concerns.[24] So, Sartre's philosophy and especially his involvement in the politics of his day appealed to a number of writers. In 1953, a French-educated Lebanese critic and writer, Suhayl Idris, founded his literary periodical, *al-Adab,* in Beirut. *Al-Adab* was a loud voice for the proponents of committed literature. In fact, Idris, in his opening remarks of the first issue, "The Message of *al-Adab,*" proclaims that the main goal of the periodical is to call for and encourage "committed" literature. The mature writers, according to Idris, are those who live and witness their era; while they reflect and express the needs of their Arab societies, they pave the way for the reformers to deal with the pressing issues of the times.[25] In brief, Idris believes in the prophetic vision and message of the writer. Commitment, as Badawi puts it, "denotes . . . a certain measure of nationalism, Arab or otherwise . . . the need for a writer to have a message, instead of just delighting in creating a work of the imagination."[26]

The decade of the 1960s witnessed political setbacks and disappointments, especially with the eruption of the 1967 Arab-Israeli war and the Israeli attack on the Beirut international airport in 1968. As Sabry Hafez observes, a new sensibility was emerging in the changing social, political, and cultural atmosphere.[27] The writers of this decade, disappointed with the social and political conditions, and especially with the artistic means employed by previous generations (mainly that of the socialist-realist trend), felt the need to renew their artistic methods, especially by moving away from the portrayal of reality as it is and starting an individual search for truth.[28] Khalida Sa`id categorizes some of the novels in this decade as novels of "protest," for they deal with rebellion against the established order or the present reality. Halim Barakat, while accepting Sa`id's classification, goes beyond her definition to call these works "novels of revolutionary change":

> *Novels of revolutionary change*
> *invalidate the hypothesis that*
> *literature reflects reality, and confirm*
> *the hypothesis of influence or the*
> *creation of a new awareness towards*
> *transcendence and a restructuring of*
> *existing arrangements. Such novels*
> *invalidate also the hypothesis that*
> *there is a conflict between art and*
> *political commitment. Literature can*
> *subordinate politics to creative and*

reflective thinking, and undertake the
task of promoting a new
consciousness.[29]

The decade of the 1970s and well into the 1980s is best analyzed by Kamal Abu-Deeb in his article "Cultural Creation in a Fragmented Society."[30] Abu-Deeb contends that Arab society in general should be analyzed within a larger picture of socioeconomic and political structures, and specifically in the context of "successive Arab failures" and the internal divisions and conflicts within the society itself. He also explains how "the characteristics of Arabic writing, particularly on the level of its structure, have been determined by an intensifying process of fragmentation in the various spheres of life."[31] This fragmentation, however, is inevitably bound to affect the formations of social and political institutions, the economic and class structure, and mainly our readings of history and tradition.

Elias Khoury's literary production should be analyzed and appreciated against such a backdrop of social and political upheavals, of fragmentations on many levels of the Lebanese state as a result of the civil war. On one hand, Khoury has to contend with writing not only about the present but also *in* the present. By this I mean he has to write in the midst of war and destruction, where writing becomes a process and a discovery of things, and not a word of gospel that embodies the absolute truth. For the moments of enunciation and/or writing about events are still in the making, shifting alliances and changing gears. On the other hand, Khoury's means of expression is Arabic, a language that is saturated with the aforementioned debates he has inherited about the function of the language. Khoury, then, has to contend with the complexity and history of the language while at the same time he needs to write about the lived experience of the present moment, that of the Lebanese civil war.

Since the eruption of the Lebanese civil war (1975-89), there has been a change in a particular discourse employed in the novel. This change in discursive practices is due to the disintegration of the social structure of the Lebanese state. With the collapse of civil society, the emergence of various political and power entities, the disappearance of a single truth, Lebanese writers have come to experience not only disappointment in the political structure and its mechanism operating in the state but also disbelief and doubt in everything that goes on around them, even disbelief in their own identity and subjectivity. That is to say, they are left with bits and pieces to draw from, and to build around them their fictional worlds in their search to comprehend the continuously changing reality. The war has imposed a new set of themes that are directly related to their historical moment. The shattered reality, the disintegrating society, the schizophrenic individual, chaos, violence, paranoia, tension, fear, death—all these themes preoccupy contemporary writers such as Ghada al-Samman, Etel `Adnan, Hanan al-Shaykh, Yusuf Habashi al-Ashqar, and Elias Khoury. War-related themes have forced them to find new ways of dealing with them.

The new form used by contemporary writers of the civil war signals the failure of the ready-made form that characterized pre–civil war novels. But this failure of the ready-made form does not signal a loss of significance. Instead, it indicates that the Lebanese novel, as a specific cultural form with a particular historical relationship to the idea of the state, is formally affected by the disintegration of the state. This formal effect is discerned in discursive change: Something is happening to the narrative itself with respect to syntax, word choice, languages employed, narrative coherence, reference, and so on. These movements of disintegration parallel, in one way or another, what is happening in the civil war; they parallel, but do not reflect as in a mirror image, the disintegration of the state. In other words, the disintegration is that of the integrity of the Lebanese novel—the traditional cohesive structure that previously dominated the novel production. In fact, this disintegration of the ready-made form allows for the emergence of a fragmentary, but more sophisticated, form.

The subject in the Lebanese novel is historically constructed as a wholesome human being. She or he is construed as a bourgeois subject or a modern subject that knows her- or himself vis-à-vis the object. That is to say, the subject knows the self in relation to the outside world that is not "me." Most of the characters presented, for example, by Ghada al-Samman, Layla 'Usayran, Emily Nassrallah, Layla Ba`lbaki, Tawfiq Yusuf `Awwad, Suhayl Idris, and Halim Barakat, are quite aware of who they are and what they want in relation to their surroundings. Each of these novelists' characters is a self-conscious knowing subject who is presented as a coherent, unified individual. Each is presented in an organized consequential order, where the logical ordering of time unfolds the construction of the subject in question.

Khoury, however, in his fictional works dismantles the traditional way of writing where cause and effect dominate the narrative structure. This dismantling, which signifies a rejection of the traditional delineation of events, presents a plunge in medias res where the beginning is mostly blurred or unknown and the ending is unclear or uncertain. Put differently, a ready-made form, with its Aristotelian prerequisites of a beginning, middle, and end, can no longer convey the complexity of the present moments lived and expressed in Khoury's fictional writings. In his novels, we do not have a logical unfolding of time or a coherent unified subject. On the contrary, time is fragmented into many times, where the past intrudes on the present or the present is intensified in a moment of pain, search, and discovery. Instead of a coherent unified subject, we have a subject that has to be constructed across time and pieced together—if such a patching is possible!—by and through language. Khoury constructs his subjects with contradictions, with competing beliefs and practices. In other words, we get a subject whose subjectivity while being constructed is called into question. Moreover, instead of an authoritative narrative voice, we have speaking subjects where singular pronouns (I, you, he, she) get mixed up, and their various positionalities interchange: "I said I'll bend down and I'll lean over and I'll go to sleep. The stranger said I'll bend down and I'll lean over and I'll go to sleep." In most of Khoury's novels, we find the narrator as a participating subject where the authority of the narrative voice disappears: "I am the one who speaks. I am the one who talked all the time."[32]

When his novel *Little Mountain* appeared in French in 1987, Khoury expressed his concern about a certain type of reader who tends to reduce any translated text to a mere historical or anthropological document of the source culture.[33] Such reductionist readings usually treat the text as a transparent cipher of political and ideological positions. Although one cannot disregard the specificity of any literary text, one should be very careful not to read a text as a mere reflection of events taking place, for example, in the streets of Beirut. Khoury's writing problematizes such readings, and his novels resist being reduced to sociological studies.

Gates of the City is the most abstract of Khoury's fictional works. It is a dreamlike novel in which the dream verges on being real, and the real becomes slippery and intangible. This dreamlike atmosphere lends *Gates of the City* to being read as a poetic text. The novel raises many issues related to love, security, search, death, authority, narration, memory, writing. These issues are only raised to be interrogated and contested.

Any reader who is used to reading novels in a traditional fashion, where the author provides answers to the questions he or she raises in the text, will be very much disappointed in *Gates of the City*. Like Khoury's other works, this novel defies summary and challenges the reader's attempt to fix its meaning in a specific fashion because of the many levels of meanings that could be negotiated. The novel does not provide us with absolute answers to the stranger's questionings and search. The stranger, who tries to ask about the city's square and gates, is surprised "to find that nobody answers his questions." He even "walked while asking," without waiting for an answer. It is significant that the stranger does not wait for the answers, because the important thing is to raise the questions and to ponder about why and how. For such questionings lead to other, more complex investigations, as the roads traveled by the stranger "led to roads and alleys ended in alleys."

Like the roads and alleys the stranger encounters, we move from one story to another that the stranger listened to as he "walked and walked." Walking, which signifies a certain kind of movement, forward or backward, becomes synonymous with questionings that also indicate a back-and-forth movement as in a dialog. Walking and questioning in this context could be easily read, however, as metaphors for writing. (I will discuss this later.)

In *Gates of the City,* as in his other fictional works, Khoury challenges the traditional narrative structure. The structure of this novel resembles that of a circle where beginning and end are hard to detect. The events are not constructed at different progressing stages as in a coherent unified narrative, but they constitute moments of disruption where each event or even each sentence could be read as a story by itself: "He was a man and he was a stranger, he doesn't remember how his story began because he doesn't know. He saw himself in the middle of the story and didn't ask how it began, because he was busy with its ending."

To keep readers from being busy with the stories' endings, Khoury usually provides us at the beginnings of his novels with what will "happen." Khalil Jaber in *The White Faces* is found dead. We try to reconstruct his life and investigate his death, as we do Gandhi's in *The Journey of Little Gandhi* after the Israelis kill him during their invasion of Beirut. We read on the first page of *Gates of the City* that the stranger "found that he didn't know the ending either, and that the others didn't know the ending, because the ending can't be known, because the ending is an ending."

In "Writing the Present," Khoury observes that Arabic creative writing has to contend with two "miracles" represented by "the bygone past and the nonexistent future," in order to be able to write the present. He demonstrates his argument with an anecdote about Abu Nuwwas and Khalaf al-Ahmar where Khalaf orders Abu Nuwwas to first memorize and then to forget what he has memorized of poetry in order to become a creative poet.[34] In this way, Khalaf prescribes two important "mirrors" — "memory and forgetfulness" — as indispensable for creative writing. It is worth quoting Khoury's argument in its entirety:

> *Literary writing is not an ordered*
> *version of reality; the story is not*
> *actually the event. It is the event in*
> *remembrance and re-creation. When*
> *the event turns into a story, it takes*
> *for itself its own history, considering*
> *it as awareness of the lived moment,*
> *at once separation from it and*
> *designation of it. This separation*
> *and designation, which we call*
> *the literary lie, is the truth. The*
> *writer does not look for the truth*
> *outside himself. The truth is not*
> *ready-made. It is made and told.*
> *Telling it is one of the forms of*
> *making it.[35]*

"Telling" a story is what really counts in narrative fiction, and not the story's "ending," for "the ending is an ending," as we read in *Gates of the City*. The significant issue is how the spoken word, that of telling, is transformed and transferred by the act of writing. Since writing, as Foucault observes, "refers not to a thing but to speech, a work of language only advances more deeply into the intangible density of the mirror, calls forth the double of this already doubled writing, discovers in this way a possible and impossible infinity, ceaselessly strives after speech, maintains it beyond the death which condemns it."[36] Writing, then, gives a story some kind of specificity in time and place, and saves it from oblivion and death. The stranger in *Gates of the City* keeps looking for his lost suitcase. The suitcase contains papers, a pen, and his father's picture. His persistent search for the suitcase signifies his urgent need to write down and register his experience so that his ordeal will not be lost in time and will not fade from memory.

Khoury's project, then, is to adopt the Arabic language and to adapt it to present times and conditions. His project is not to disregard classical Arabic, but rather to make it more accessible to the immediate lived moments and experiences. This is not a discrediting of the past but rather a dialog or negotiation with it. Writing in this context comes closer to the daily uttered words and narrated stories. In Khoury's fictional world, we move from one story to another as if we are reading stories in *A Thousand and One Nights* within the context of the Lebanese civil war. The traditional form of *alf layla wa-layla* is appropriated from the past to fit the needs and concerns of the present.

Writing in and about the war is Khoury's project so as to register the experience of the present and prevent its lessons from being forgotten in the future. Yet, at the same time, writing does not refer to one specific thing; it refers to itself and to the act of writing itself. Put differently, writing becomes a mirror that does not reflect a single absolute truth or reality. Like the mirror, it approaches reality from many different angles, as the opening verse by Ibn `Arabi in Khoury's *Little Gandhi* tells us: "The face is one except when reflected by many mirrors, then it becomes many." Many of the questions, images, metaphors, and themes appear constantly in Khoury's fictional writings. For example, are the circles the stranger draws in sand connected to the circle in *The Circle*?[37] Does *The Circle* anticipate *Gates of the City* by explicitly stating that "there is a gate or several gates for every city"? Or does it anticipate *Little Gandhi,* where we find the same image of "black rain"? Is the odor that permeates Khoury's collection *Subject and Predicate* the same odor that keeps recurring in most of his other works? Is the white with which Khalil Jaber in *The White Faces* paints the city walls the same white that we encounter in *Gates of the City* and other novels?[38] What is the significance of the number seven (seven gates, seven circles, seven women, many of Khoury's novels consist of seven chapters)?[39] Is it accidental that characters in *Gates of the City* possess no names and are sometimes featureless, while some characters in *Gandhi* have more than one name?

These recurrences or repetitions in Khoury's writings suggest his preoccupation with such issues. As Edward Said tells us in his introduction to *Little Mountain,* it is "as if the narrator needed reiteration to prove to himself that improbable things actually *did* take place." For how can a novelist write about the present with all its contradictions and inherited problems from the past, and have a ready-made or an already fabricated solution? Writing about the present, and in this context the Lebanese civil war, has become an exploration and a discovery, as Khoury puts it, "towards the known and the unknown. . . .

Writing indicates a way of life and not a lesson filled with ideology."[40] Writing itself is a journey like the physical or metaphorical journeys traveled by the stranger, Gandhi, Khalil Jaber, Mansour, and others in Khoury's fictional worlds.

As I have noted here, *Gates of the City* negotiates its meanings.[41] There are many more possible readings of this novel that I have not touched on. I would like to conclude, however, with one of these readings. When Kamal Boullata, a Palestinian visual artist and poet, was asked to provide drawings to accompany the publication in 1981 of *Abwab al-Madina,* he wrote "An Introduction to the Atmosphere of E.E.K.: Text and Drawings in Reading *Gates of the City,*" which appeared in *Mawaqif* in the same year. The Arabic pronunciation of Khoury's abbreviated name produces "Akh," a sound usually uttered when one is in pain. The pain Boullata experienced on reading the novel produced a text and illustrations that should be read as an extension of Khoury's novel. A few translated lines from Boullata's text will also serve the reader well in illuminating the complexity of *Gates of the City*:

> *He is me, and I am the first woman,*
> *and he is the gate-woman, and I am*
> *the city gate, and the city is the*
> *grave, and the grave is me. . . . At the*
> *city gate, beggars recite the verses of*
> *Proust and know not that Zeno's*
> *time has begun.*[42]

Notes

1. Roger Allen, *The Arabic Novel: An Historical and Critical Introduction* (Syracuse, N.Y.: Syracuse University Press, 1982), pp. 15-18; Edward Said, introduction to Halim Barakat, *Days of Dust*, trans. Trevor Le Gassick (Wilmette, Ill.: Medina University Press International, 1974), p. xiii.

2. Marun `Abbud, *Ruwwad al-Nahda* (Beirut: Dar al-Thaqafa, 1966), p. 184. Marun `Abbud (1886-1962) was a Lebanese novelist, short-story writer, and critic.

3. Said, introduction to Barakat, *Days of Dust*, p. xiii.

4. Roger Allen states that "while the novel tradition has indeed drawn most of its inspiration from Western models, a number of writers and especially critics have been reinvestigating the nature of narrative in the mediaeval tradition of popular prose" (*The Arabic Novel*, p. 18).

5. Allen, ibid.; `Ali `Atwi, *Tatawwur Fann al-Qissa al-Lubnaniyya al-`Arabiyya* (Beirut: Dar al-Afaq, 1982); `Abdul Muhsin Badr, *Tatawwur al-Riwayah al-`Arabiyya* (Cairo: Dar al-Ma`arif, 1962); Suhayl Idris, *al-Qissa fi Lubnan* (Cairo: Arab League's Institute of Higher Education, 1958); Muhammad Nejm, *al-Qissa fi al-Adab al-`Arabi al-Hadith*, 3rd ed. (Beirut: Dar al-Thaqafa, 1966).

6. Allen, *The Arabic Novel*, pp. 19 and 46-98.

7. Badr, *Tatawwur al-Riwayah*, p. 119.

8. E.g., Jurji Zaydan, Ya`qub Sarruf, Khalil Mutran, Farah Antun, Jubran Khalil Jubran, Mayy Ziadeh, and others.

9. Badr, *Tatawwur al-Riwayah*, p. 32.

10. Karam Milhem Karam started writing stories in 1928. Nejm considers him to be the pioneer of the modern Arabic Lebanese novel (Nejm, *al-Qissa fi al-Adab*, pp. 31, 34). By 1931, Karam had nearly 200 stories—translations, adaptations, and creative fiction—published in his periodical *Alf Layla wa-Layla*. See `Atwi, *Tatawwur Fann al-Qissa*, p. 73.

11. Nejm, *al-Qissa fi al-Adab*, p. 32.

12. `Abbas Mahmud al-`Aqqad and Ibrahim al-Mazini are Egyptian novelists and essayists. They are known as al-Diwanists for their two-volume combined work on criticism and literature.

13. David Semah, *Four Egyptian Literary Critics* (Leiden: Brill, 1974), p. 13.

14. Introduction to Mikha'il Nu`aymah's *al-Ghirbal* (Cairo: Dar al-Ma`arif, n.d.), pp. 7-8.

15. Semah, *Four Egyptian Literary Critics*, p. 80.

16. Jabra I. Jabra, "Modern Arabic Literature and the West," in *Critical Perspectives in Modern Arabic Literature,* ed. Issa Boullata (Washington, D.C.: Three Continents Press, 1980), p. 10.

17. Semah, *Four Egyptian Literary Critics,* p. 93.

18. Muhammad Husayn Haykal, *Thawrat al-Adab* (Cairo: al-Nahda al-Misriyya, 1965), pp. 37-38.

19. Semah, *Four Egyptian Literary Critics,* p. 120 n. 1.

20. Ibid., 197.

21. Badawi in *Critical Perspectives,* p. 34.

22. Muhammad Barrada, *Muhammad Mandur wa Tanzir al-Naqd al-`Arabi* (Beirut: Dar al-Adab, 1979), p. 208.

23. Jabra in *Critical Perspectives,* p. 19.

24. Robert C. Solomon, *Continental Philosophy since 1750: The Rise and Fall of the Self* (Oxford and New York: Oxford University Press, 1988), p. 177.

25. Suhayl Idris, *Mawaqif wa-Qadaya Adabiyya* (Beirut: Dar al-Adab, 1977), p. 9.

26. Badawi, *Critical Perspectives,* p. 24.

27. Sabry Hafez, "The Egyptian Novel in the Sixties," in *Critical Perspectives,* p. 171.

28. Khalida Sa`id, *Harakiyyat al-Ibda`: Dirasat fi al-Adab al-`Arabi al-Hadith* (Beirut: Dar al-`Awda, 1979), p. 213.

29. Halim Barakat, "Arabic Novels and Social Transformation," in *Studies in Modern Arabic Literature,* ed. R. C. Ostle (Warminster: Aris & Phillips, 1975), p. 137.

30. Kamal Abu-Deeb, "Cultural Creation in a Fragmented Society," in *The Next Arab Decade: Alternative Futures,* ed. Hisham Sharabi (Boulder, Colo.: Westview Press, 1988), pp.160-81.

31. Abu-Deeb, ibid., p.160.

32. See my article on *Rihlat Ghandi al-Saghir* forthcoming in *Mawaqif,* 1993. This novel will be published in English translation as *The Journey of Little Gandhi* by the University of Minnesota Press in 1993.

33. An interview with Elias Khoury in *Al-Nahar al-`Arabi wal-Dawli,* May 25, 1987.

34. Al-Ahmar was a poet and critic during the `Abbasid period.

35. "Kitabat al-Hadir," in *al-Safir,* October 11, 1986. Khoury translated this article into English; it appeared in *Emergences,* the journal of the Group for the Study of Composite Cultures (2 [Spring 1990], p. 9).

36. Michel Foucault, *Language, Counter-Memory, Practice,* ed. Donald F. Bouchard (Ithaca, N.Y.: Cornell University Press, 1977), p. 56.

37. Khoury published his first novel `An `Alaqat al-Da'ira (About the interrelatedness of the circle) at the beginning of 1975, i.e., just before the

outbreak of the Lebanese civil war. It was as if his piercing insight and sensibility made Khoury aware of the country's destiny. His second novel, *Little Mountain,* appeared in 1977; it was published in English translation by the University of Minnesota Press in 1989. In 1981, Khoury published two novels, *Gates of the City* and *The White Faces.* The latter appeared in French in 1992. Then came *Al-Mubtada' wal-Khabar* (Subject and predicate, 1984), *Little Gandhi* in 1989, and *Mamlakat al-Ghuraba'* (The kingdom of the strangers) in 1993.

38. See my review of *Al-Wujuh al-Bayda'* for the significance of "white" in *Jusur; UCLA Journal of Middle Eastern Studies,* 4 (1988), 94-97.

39. Abu-Deeb discusses how the semiotic system of traditional culture is emptied of its traditional meaning in contemporary writings; "Cultural Creation in a Fragmented Society," p. 173.

40. Elias Khoury, "The Unfolding of Modern Fiction and Arab Memory," *MMLA,* 23 (1990), p. 7.

41. For example, does the dead king in *Gates of the City* represent authority that is no more? If yes, then what do we make of the wailing women? Are they wailing for the absence of authority, or are they afraid of facing something new — the unknown?

42. Kamal Boullata, "An Introduction to the Atmosphere of E.E.K.: Text and Drawings in Reading *Gates of the City,*" *Mawaqif,* 41-42 (Spring-Summer 1981), pp. 89-96.

GATES OF THE CITY

Beginning

He was a man and he was a stranger,

He didn't tell his story to anyone, he didn't know he was a story to be told. He thought, he used to think, the way we think, and he was like everyone was, but he didn't tell anyone, because he didn't know that the things that had happened could be told to anyone.

He was a man and he was a stranger,

He doesn't remember how his story began, because he doesn't know. He saw himself in the middle of the story and didn't ask how it began, because he was busy with its ending. And when the ending came he found that he didn't know the ending either, and that the others didn't know the ending, because the ending can't be known, because the ending is an ending.

He was a man and he was a stranger,

There he walks and walks, he asks and asks, and I'm the one who saw him. I didn't see him there and I didn't see him here, I spotted him and I approached him, he was walking and walking, the roads were an extension of his emaciated, collapsing body, but he went farther away. He didn't know more than a few useless words, but they were his words. What does a man do with his words if they aren't useful for anything? He didn't ask that question, because he was walking, and his words were walking along with him, and breaking down with him and falling as if they were leaves falling from the branches of an old tree.

He was a man and like a man he walked,

Like a man he walked to his death, he saw his death close at hand, but he walked. He was walking and asking and no one answered, then he stopped and started answering, he didn't know the answer but he answered anyway.

It was said that he burned, and it was said that he melted on the grave and it was said. But the city he came to from faraway places vanished. It was said that it had sunk in the eyes, and it was said that it had gone to the sea and it was said that it had caught fire in the forest and it was said. But it vanished and the search for it was no longer possible, the city was no longer possible and the man was no longer.

He was a man and like a man he walked,

Like a man he walked to his death, but I spotted him, but I tried to approach him, but I tried to say to him, I saw him in the distance, and like the distance he was, like a point turning into angles, and like an angle turning into circles, and like a circle shrinking into a distant point.

And in the distance, he was a point that melts and melts but doesn't disappear. He was a hand cut up into hands that don't vanish. It was he, a man and a stranger, walking to his death.

The stranger walked and walked.

And beside him walked another man.

And beside the other man walked another.

And they all walked to the faraway city, and in the faraway city they lit a fire, and in the fire they die, and in the fire they are afraid, and in the fire they write a story that

4

begins where it should have ended, and when it ends it is as though it never began.

And the storyteller tells what he saw, and the storyteller bears witness to what he witnessed, and the witness dies as the victims die, and the witness knows no more than walls and doors and eyes in which hands burn, and hands that stretch out to smoldering eyes.

And the one who witnessed writes about his eyes, and walks beside the man who walked and doesn't leave him alone and he will not be except where he found himself.

I

The Stranger

The man was standing in front of the walls of the big city. He didn't know how to enter, but he had arrived. The journey was long and exhausting. Innumerable days and nights of cold and rain and exposure to the elements. But he finally arrived. He was carrying papers, pencils, and notebooks. He looked at the walls of the city, he saw nothing but walls, he didn't hear a sound. So he almost cried. He stood all alone. He put on the ground a suitcase full of things that no longer had any meaning and sat. He waited for someone to come. For men or women to come and welcome him, to show him how to enter. That is what he had dreamed. He dreamed that when he arrived at that faraway city someone would come who would take him by the hand and lead him into a bath of marble and warmth, and dress him in the most beautiful clothes. He dreamed of beautiful women and the fragrance of perfume and flowers. He dreamed of mothers and mistresses.

But he stood all alone, and sat all alone, and grieved all alone.

Then the man decided to walk around the walls. He carried his suitcase and his exhausted body and walked. The walls were naked and high. The smell of earth and cement. He didn't see one tree, and he didn't touch grass or flowers. He walked a long time and walked. Then he saw an elevated gate. The heavy iron gate stood in the middle of the wall as though it were guarding the city. He stopped in front of the door and shouted. He said he had come from a distant place. And he said he wanted to enter. But he didn't hear any answer. Even the echo of his voice didn't come back to him. Then a young woman appeared. She was more beautiful than all the other women. She wore a long purple dress, and on her head was a white scarf that glimmered as if it were a halo of light. She approached him, she took him by the hand, and said things the man doesn't remember well. But he remembers that he experienced an all-encompassing feeling of joy. He experienced that kind of feeling that issues forth from your head to your toes in one burst, so that it makes you quiver like the trunk of a ripe tree, then the fruits fall from the tree onto the ground and the children pick them up. The man quivered like a tree trunk, but the fruit didn't fall and the children didn't dance around him with joy, and the tree was not a tree.

And what the man tries to remember of that beautiful woman's words now appears obscure. But he does remember that she said she would open the door for him, and he must enter, but she refused to enter with him. You go in first, then when you reach the middle of the city you'll see a door of gold. Go in without knocking on the door, and there you'll find me waiting for you.

The man thought. Then he felt afraid and said no.

He picked up his suitcase and walked. The wall was round. The man felt that it was circling around the earth. He walked and walked. He felt lonely and empty. He regretted not entering, then he walked. And suddenly he saw an elevated gate standing in the middle of the wall. He knocked on the door no one opened it, then a young woman more beautiful than the first appeared before him. She took him by the hand, and she spoke beautiful words, she said she'd open the city gate for him, but she wouldn't go in with him. And there in the middle of the city you'll see a door of silver. Enter without knocking on the door, and there you'll find me waiting for you.

But the man who had spent all those long days searching for the city felt afraid.

How can I enter alone? I won't go in.

And he walked.

The wall was round, the man walked and days followed nights on top of his exhausted body. But he was walking and that elevated door was walking around him. He felt thirsty. He remembered water he dreamed of, and the water had a color. That was how he dreamed. He enters the city and finds water white like milk, but it tastes like water. You drink but you don't quench your thirst, the water doesn't run dry and you don't quench your thirst and you drink.

The man walked around the wall and walked. And he saw a third gate and a fourth and a fifth and a sixth. And in front of every gate stood a woman more beautiful than the one before her. And he feels all-encompassing joy, but he refuses to enter because he is afraid.

He had walked endless periods of time. And he walked all alone. And now how could he enter all alone? Maybe the people of the city thought he was a stranger or a thief or a bandit. He wouldn't enter except in the company of a beautiful woman. He wouldn't enter except handsome like a prince. That was how he dreamed while he crossed the mountains and slept out in the open. And he asks the birds about this city, and when he arrives at its walls, he doesn't find anyone who wants to enter with him. He finds only promises and words.

He said I won't enter and he walked.

The man began to stumble. Hunger and thirst and the oppression of long days, he felt as though diseases were penetrating his bones, he felt as though his bones were about to collapse, and he remembered the tree, and how he always imagined that man is a tree full of branches. He felt afraid and almost fell to the ground, and when he saw the seventh gate he felt incapable of continuing to run around the wall. He stopped in front of the iron door and shouted. So a young woman came, and she spoke words resembling the words of the first woman. She spoke about a door of gold, and about water and warmth. She asked him to walk in. And in the middle of the city he'd find the door, and he must enter, and she'd be waiting there for him.

The man didn't think long, he agreed, but he told the woman he felt a little bit afraid. So she put a tender hand on his head and smiled, and he felt as though he had the whole world in his hands. He felt strong like an untamed horse. He felt he'd reached the city, and he'd be the first to discover the door that leads to a huge palace that never ends.

The woman opened the city gate, but she wasn't holding a key in her hand. She approached the gate and touched it with her beautiful hand. The gate opened and the man went in. And as he was about to look behind him, to thank her, and to confirm his date with her, the gate had already closed, and there was no longer anything but the clanging of the iron banging in his ears.

The man entered. He saw houses of clay and concrete. He smelled the odor of people and he remembered his own odor. Because of the intensity of his intimacy with his body, over those long distances, he had forgotten that people have an odor. He felt that the smell of people is more beautiful than the smell of flowers and grass. But no one turned to look at him.

He said never mind, tomorrow they'll know. He smiled like someone hiding a big secret that will inevitably be revealed, and he walked.

He remembered that the woman told him to walk along the straight road and he'd reach the city square, where he'd find the golden door.

He walked and walked.

And he didn't find the city square. The roads led to roads and the alleys ended in alleys. He tried to ask, but he was surprised that no one would answer his questions.

He asked a man, the man looked at him a long time and walked.

He asked a woman, she didn't stop to hear his question.

The stranger felt that he was a stranger in his own city. But he decided to pursue the journey and pursue the question. I have arrived, and I won't return before I enter that door, or before I sleep with that woman, or before I drink from that water.

He walked as he asked, and he no longer waited for the answer, he began asking as he walked without stopping in front of them. He became like them.

The stranger thought he had come to resemble the people of this city. Then he felt tired and exhausted. So he sat on a rock. For countless nights the man hadn't slept. And for long days he hadn't had anything to drink.

He was sitting. He looked at nothing and didn't see anything, when an old man resembling the forefathers came. He sat beside him and said to him, "I know you're looking for the city square. Get up and follow me."

"But who are you?"

"Me, I'm the one who guides strangers to the city square, this is my profession. For a thousand years while I have been living here, I don't die because no one in the city has wanted to learn my profession, do you want to learn this profession? My body has longed for the earth, and my bones yearn for rest."

"No," shouted the stranger. "I want to go to the city square."

The hunchbacked old man walked in front of him, and the stranger walked behind, then the old man stopped and said here, and left.

The square was big. A white square, with white dirt and white sky. But the stranger didn't find a door and he didn't find women.

He proceeded to the middle of the square, where the white stones glimmered. He saw a coffin of stone, inside it was a corpse of stone. And he heard sounds of wailing and weeping.

He turned but didn't see anyone. He threw his suitcase on the ground and it split open. He sat then he stood then he sat.

"But where are the women?"

The stranger decided to leave the city. This is not a city. He left his torn suitcase and walked. Then he saw seven women on the outskirts of the square, with their long hair and dirty fingernails, weeping in a semicircle.

He asked and asked.

A woman turned to him and said they were weeping over the king of the city who was dead, and who was sleeping in his coffin.

He asked them. He said that he remembered. This

woman was standing at the gate. He asked her about her promise. Then he asked her to guide him to the city gate.

The women's wailing increased. The first woman said to him that she doesn't remember that the city has a gate. Then she said she doesn't remember the presence of a wall.

He left them and walked. He ran. The roads led to roads, and alleys ended in alleys, and he didn't find the gate or the wall.

And when the man returned to the square, he felt that his home was here.

The stranger looked off into the distance and didn't see anything. He was listening to distant wailing.

He remembered that in his ripped suitcase there were papers and pencils. So he went to search for his suitcase.

II

The Search for the Suitcase

I said I'll bend down and I'll lean over and I'll go to sleep.

The stranger said I'll bend down and I'll lean over and I'll go to sleep. The stranger looked, the square was white. Nothing but whiteness. The stranger felt white fear, he was afraid of meeting the old man who resembles the forefathers. He was afraid because he remembers, now he remembers, the old man had no eyes. The man stands in the middle of the white square, he is afraid, he feels tired, but when he passes his hand across his forehead to wipe away the sweat he discovers that there is no sweat, and that the fear comes from the sight of the old man. He remembers, a wide forehead full of white hair, a face that disappears behind dark lines, sparse hair that wraps around the face and scatters about like the wind. Then no, not possible to, perhaps, or. The stranger felt the need for screams to come out of his throat. Then he decided to bend down, then how can a man not have two eyes like all other men? How can it not be, he doesn't know, or how did he lead me across streets that don't end, and how did he take me to a white square, and how did I smell a white scent?

The stranger felt his body lengthening in the wind, he

looked at his hands and saw them stretching, and the square started getting smaller and narrower before his eyes. The man stretched out his hands and rubbed his eyes and he heard a strange sound coming from his eyelids as they came into contact with his fingers. He felt very sleepy. Sleep will come and inhabit his body, and he felt as though he could stretch over an endless white space.

The man fell down, his feet staggered beneath the rustle of drowsiness. He fell lower, and lower was deep, he fell more and began to stretch, the white was disappearing and darkness was spreading. The stranger said I'll bend down and I'll lean over and I'll go to sleep. The bright whiteness, like that of an egg, began to circle around the egg. Light darkness penetrated by the dust. The man tried to close his eyes but the dust danced under lights that came and crisscrossed in his eyes. Dust that resembles dust.

The man saw and shut his eyes, he tried to shut his eyes, he stood, he tried to stand, he bent down, he tried to bend down. He said things he doesn't remember well. He told stories about eyes that don't close and the city whose seven gates he came to and whose square he didn't find. And when he did find its square he lost its gates and when he returned to the square he lost his suitcase and when he found his suitcase he lost the woman, and when the woman, the woman said, then he found himself standing all alone in the middle of the white square that had a white stone coffin in its center, and the man goes back to the square and searches for a suitcase he lost.

How do I search for the suitcase?

The man said he doesn't know the directions in this city, for the light emanates from the middle of the square. How can I distinguish the directions? And the suitcase was with me when I stood next to the old man, where was the old man standing and where was I standing? The man decided to circle around the stone coffin. He said I'll make a mark on the dirt of the square and go around, and when I get to the mark I will have returned to where I started from. The man knelt down, he stuck his finger in the sand and drew a circle then he drew another circle behind it, he drew a third circle, he drew seven circles and looked ahead and walked. The white sand was rising up between his feet without making any noise. The man looked into the distance and the distance got farther away and the coffin was still far off in the middle of a circle that got wider and wider. The stranger walked and walked, he looked and he didn't see, but he was walking. And suddenly he saw black dots in the distance shimmering amidst the whiteness, and he couldn't make out are they birds searching for something in the sand? He came close to them but after he had traveled for hours and hours he felt as though he was getting farther away from them. The man thought that they weren't birds, how can the birds not fly in this city? He remembered that he had read stories about birds that talk and birds that don't fly. And he decided to walk in the direction of the black dots. But he was afraid of getting lost. He said how will I know how to get back to where I am? He leaned over onto the ground and drew seven circles around the sand with his finger. He said when I find the dots I'll return to my place and resume my walk around the coffin. And the man walked in the direction of the black dots and walked innumerable days. And the lights of the dust came and crisscrossed in his eyes then disappeared, and the man didn't feel sleepy, he felt a bit thirsty, he felt that water, he no longer remembers how he imagined the water and he said that water resembles a discarded body, but he was unable to express more than that. He said I can bear the thirst and when I arrive I'll find that water. And the man walked, there were no roads in the square, the man walked and he didn't walk on roads, and there was dust flying or something white that looked like dust, something fine flying in particles that glimmered under a light emanating from the ground of the big square.

And after hours or days the man arrived. He began to see the dots getting bigger, he said I've arrived, and he walked, the dots got smaller, but he continued on, and they got bigger again. And when they began to grow and grow the man suddenly felt tired and said I'll bend down, but he continued on. And when he arrived he saw the black dots turning into seven dots, and the dot is a woman or looks like a woman. The man drew near and saw seven women wearing mourning clothes and walking one behind the other. He tried to ask, he said they must know something about the suitcase. He drew near and opened his mouth and said, but his voice didn't come out of his mouth. He tried again, and he put his hands on his ears and opened his mouth and said, but the words don't come out, and the women walk around the square. He walked behind them, he tried to proceed, he said I'll reach the last woman and touch her maybe she'll turn to me or maybe or. But he advances and the women advance. He sped up but he couldn't, he felt but he didn't know, he said but his voice didn't come out. The man felt a desire for eyes. The women stopped. He came closer and opened his mouth and shouted. And he heard a sound like the creaking of an old rusty door. He raised his voice more and the sound transformed into something like moaning. He tried to ask. And suddenly he heard and it was as though the entire square had become one vast ear and the moaning of the women rose faintly. He talked and moaning came out of his mouth as though his mouth had changed into a well. The woman sat, her black robe spreading over the sand. He sat next to her and tried and he saw her looking, he looked and saw the six women walking, he pointed to her, he spoke, his voice began to come back, he asked the woman about the suitcase and the woman said, she lifted her black garment off her face and he saw the whiteness. It was the white of the eye in the shape of an oval face, a mouth as though it were drawn on the face, two dots in the place of eyes and whiteness. He heard words, the words weren't coming from the woman's mouth but from her stomach, the woman said she waited for him a long time.

"I waited but you didn't come."

"I came and I didn't find anyone."

She indicated with the edge of her robe and said that she was waiting for him in the palace where the white bath and steam are, I waited for you behind the door, but when you arrived at the door you stopped and you didn't knock or try to enter.

There wasn't a door, the man said.

"And you were next to a man I don't know, and you were talking, I tried to wave to you but you didn't look."

The man felt the world was breaking into tiny particles that were planting themselves in the grains of sand that covered the square. He asked the woman about the wall and about the gates, and he heard moaning, he looked and saw the procession of black dots approaching him, and a second woman sitting next to the first woman while the procession moved. He asked the woman about the suitcase. She lifted her garment off her face and he saw the whiteness. A white eye that elongates and becomes a face, two black dots on the uppermost part of the face, and a black mouth as if it were drawn with a fine pen. And he heard the answers. The woman said the door was made of gold and she asked him why he didn't go in. The stranger felt tears coming out of his shoulders. He said he was looking for the suitcase, so the woman pointed, and the man looks at the two women then at three women, and the women are black dots circling around the stone coffin. The sound of weeping and wailing. The man said I'll bend down and I'll lean over and I'll go to sleep. The man said the black dots are faces and the faces are like eggs. He raised his hand, stretched out his finger, and tried to touch the face, when he heard the wailing and saw another woman sitting next to the women, and the dots circling around.

And when the man sat among seven women, he felt happy, now he can ask. He stretched his finger to the egg, stretched out his hand and shouted, and something sticky came out onto his finger then the faces fell to the ground and the women's wailing increased, and the whiteness flowed onto the sand.

The black dots got up in a hurry, and faint wailing rose, and the women walked. And the stranger decided to remain in his place, he put his face between his hands and thought about crying. He heard rattling in the throat, so he lifted his face and saw the first woman standing in front of him and ordering him in a loud voice to get up. He got up, she asked him, he answered her that he was looking for the suitcase.

I left my papers in it and a picture of my father and a pencil and round pieces the man said.

The woman stands and her long hair covers her face, hair full of wrinkles and dust. She said she remembers the suitcase was someplace. She walked and he walked behind her and she came to a place and said let's dig here. He dug and didn't find anything. She walked and he walked behind her then she sat and said let's dig again. He dug and didn't find anything. Seven times she walked and seven times he walked behind her, and the seventh time she said here, he said here, and he dug and didn't find anything.

The woman cried and pointed to the women.

Why? asked the man.

She said that she left the city and came to the square, and that she had vowed to mourn for the king.

"But where is the king?"

"He's inside the stone coffin."

"Why?"

"The king ordered the city to choose seven virgins to weep over his grave, and when one of them dies she is buried next to him and is replaced by another virgin."

And she said she has been here for a thousand years. Thousands of virgins had died but she doesn't die. And that she had a dream that she won't die unless a stranger makes love to her. The woman took off her robe and said to him that all the men refuse. The stranger looked and saw breasts dangling all over her body, and he saw black dots moving in the middle of a body full of hair.

He said he was afraid.

She came closer to him.

He said he couldn't.

And the woman would get closer and the stranger couldn't. He told her that he had walked a lot and was very tired and that he couldn't. And the woman would get closer and the man tried to get farther away. Then he saw tiny worms coming out of the woman's insides and spreading all over the sand, then they started crawling on the soles of the man's feet. The man screamed and dug a hole and said I will die. He dug and the naked woman started getting dressed.

The woman said and pointed to remnants of old leather. She said that these were the remains of the suitcase and the suitcase was inside the stone coffin.

How can I get to it? the man asked.

You can't, the woman answered. You must walk to where the coffin is, and there try to climb up, but the side of the coffin is raised up a little.

The woman had put her clothes on and covered her face and left. The man dug in the ground and he saw worms coming up out of the hole and spreading all over the white square. The man remembered that he forgot to bring food with him. And he walked in the direction of the coffin.

The man walked a long time and he walked. And when he arrived he heard the women's voices, and saw the women sitting next to the stone coffin in a semicircle. He approached them and asked them about his friend. He remembered that he didn't know her name, but he asked about the one who told him about the suitcase inside the coffin.

The woman got up and the other women followed her and they approached him. The woman signaled with her hand toward the bottom of the stone coffin and he saw the remains of papers.

These are my papers, the man said.

He bent down and found that the words had been erased. He found some letters, he searched among the torn papers for his name and stumbled upon some discarded letters on the edges of torn papers.

The man sat, but the suitcase.

The woman approached him and held his hand and signaled for him to follow her.

"To where?"

The woman didn't answer and walked, and the man walked behind her. She sat so he sat next to her, and his voice mingled with the voices of the women weeping over the king.

III

The Coffin and the King

The man said to the man, he looked he didn't find a man next to him but he said it is the king, and these things that look like flowers are his coffin.

And the man was alone, and the flowers looked like his memory. Lumps of torn papers and a scent. It was the scent of memory.

The stranger's head dangles down and his extremities fall onto the fine sand and ask. And the old man who looks like the forefathers couldn't answer because he was absent and far away. And the woman who kissed him seven times on his forehead, she was the one who said to him. But now he doesn't remember what she said, but he does remember the scent, the scent of dead flowers thrown on the side of the road. And the man remembered that there are no roads in the square and that he can't bend down over the flowers to smell them. And the scent came near his nose and his mouth, then it entered his chest and spread. The man sat all alone, and he sat on the ground, and the white dust rose high up, and he was like one who becomes interconnected with dust and becomes dust, he tried to open his eyes, he couldn't. How can I see? I don't see. He tried to. But the woman who was next to him rose high up, he tried to rise up, and he said I can't, she whispered something, she held some sand and sprinkled it over the man's head and body, and the head rose and he looked high up.

And high up, in white space, a black dot got higher and higher, circling around the grave and around the square and got closer. The man said it was getting closer, he said he was afraid, he said about the bird that goes high up, he said this is a wild bird that will eat your eyes, the bird came closer and dust rose up in the shape of a pillar connecting the earth to the sky.

The man said and looked, and he saw voices in the form of little birds hovering over his head. He said that he was afraid and that he wanted to. The woman took him by the hand and he walked next to her. He wanted to ask her about the women and she put her finger over his mouth and walked. The man saw a deep hole, he sat next to it.

"This is the king," she said.

He looked at the woman and he saw her receding and changing into a distant dot. He wanted to follow her but he couldn't get up. He looked at the hole and he saw a coffin of stone, and lots of stones scattered about.

He said I'll go down to where the king is, he said I'll search there, he said there I'll find or maybe. He began and it was as though he was sliding, he felt the dust was rising from his nose and he wished. And he fell down slowly as though he were collapsing piece by piece.

The man found himself all alone and he found the king. It wasn't a king, it was a coffin of stone sealed with a white rock and on top of the cover was a corpse or the statue of a man holding his beard with his right hand and his left leg was broken, and the other hand stretched the length of his body. He got closer to it, he bent down, he knelt, and he felt a need for water.

The man tried to remember the city gates, but he forgot what color they were, he thought about the women but he forgot the color of their eyes, he thought about his suitcase but he forgot why he was searching for it, he thought about the letters he found but he forgot why he found them, and the man said that memory resembles flowers and he sat on the edge of the coffin waiting and he saw.

The man said when he opened his eyes and he saw the bird coming near his head that he had had a dream. It was the king, the king opened the door of the coffin and got up, he didn't resemble the picture that was lying on the coffin, an old man and coughing and creaking bones.

The king sat on a chair and around him sat the ministers and chamberlains. The king coughed and they fell silent and remained silent.

Why are you quiet? said the king.

They bowed down and they spoke. Then he raised his hand and everyone left. The king called out at the top of his lungs and out came a voice with distinct features, and she entered.

A woman made of yogurt. White, long hair reaching her ankles and hanging freely, and walking on the tips of her toes. Colorful clothes and surging eyes, she kissed the king's feet and sat down, she held a lute and sang and played, her voice was sad and the tune came out of her fingers and enveloped the hall and the body. He said enough. The playing and the singing stopped. He called out, and men came and locked the doors. He coughed and drank from a pitcher next to him, she got up and started dancing and swaying, he approached her and ripped her clothes and she trembled as she swayed, she bent her long neck and her eyes scattered about the expanse of the hall.

He came closer, his panting increased, and his face, I saw his face, it was like one who tries or one who doesn't want. Her laughter increased and it resounded in the middle of his face, and his face didn't resemble anything. The faces of kings don't resemble anything, the man thought. Her eyes widened and his eyes filled with tears. She sat, bent over his feet, and kissed them, she bent over and the wailing increased. He kicked her face, he raised both of his hands and went toward her, she ran away, she tried to run away.

The doors were locked and the guards were at the door and the king. He went closer. Don't kill me, she shouted, I'm yours. His eyes filled with tears and he came closer.

But is it you? the man asked.

She said yes.

And you stood at one of the gates at the wall.

She said yes.

And I saw you crying with the weeping women.

She said yes.

He said why?

She said yes.

The stranger bent down around the coffin as though he was looking for something, then he heard a voice telling him to kiss the king's hand, he kissed the hand that was holding the beard, he bent down farther and began circling around the coffin, and he saw horses, three horses and three knights and shimmering swords, the knights' faces were broad, covered with tattoos and they ran about making strange sounds. The first knight dismounts and the other two follow, he bends down, they bend down, he returns to his horse and remains motionless like stone. The

34

stranger comes close to him, he comes closer speaks to him and the knight doesn't answer.

The man circles around and sees three women carrying a large animal on their shoulders and walking. The road is long, the stranger thinks. But the women don't turn to look at anyone.

"But where are you going?"

One woman says, and her voice resembles a voice the man has heard before but he no longer remembers whose, we are offering the sacrifice to the king.

The woman doesn't say anything, she walks on and the animal's body moves forward, and women move, and the animal walks to its death.

The man circles around, and he sees a man carrying a spear with a small snake on its tip. The snake opens its mouth and wraps its tail around the head of the spear, and the man with his spear walks. He thinks that he will not ask him anything, since no one answers. All of a sudden the snake jumps from the top of the spear and the spear bows down and the man carrying it bows down and the women bow down. As for the king, he remains stretched out on his wooden bed as if he doesn't see. A woman comes from the edge of the stone coffin, she catches the snake with her hand and puts it back on top of the spear. The one holding the spear bows his head a little and continues on his way.

The stranger feels fatigue rolling down his back am I afraid? And why am I afraid? A dead king and stones with moving forms. The stranger trembles, he feels like he has become a deep valley, the abyss opens deeper but where shall the man shout . . . He hears clamor, he looks up and sees the distant bird coming near. Its wings are long and far away and its head hangs down low. The flapping of the wings spreads the smell of dead flowers throughout the grave, and the women's wailing increases. Why doesn't he come here and sit next to me? I accept, the stranger said, I accept, I will weep over the king and die for the king. But no response. Alone the distant bird comes near, raging wind and the sounds of water splashing. The man shut his eyes and leaned over the snake and he heard a hissing sound getting louder and a voice rising up. He tried to lie down next to the coffin, he tried to.

Then he heard a voice and saw a man. The lid of the stone coffin had been moved and an old man was sitting on the edge of the coffin. He opens his mouth and tries to speak. This is the king, the man thought, I must bow down.

"No need to trouble yourself," the king said. "Come and sit next to me."

"But I want to," the man said.

"No need for wanting, I've become old and these things no longer concern me."

"But they are up there, don't you hear?"

"That is up there, come and sit next to me."

The man said that he wanted to return and go with the woman. The king began to cry. But kings don't cry, thought the stranger. And the king talked about other kings, and about his back, which was hunched over from so much bowing down, but kings don't bow down, the man said, and about the corpses of the slain that are becoming more numerous, but kings . . . and about returning to the city, the stranger felt regretful, he felt he was making a mistake and that he shouldn't talk with the king, the king said and pointed to the bird, now it will descend upon us and circle around in endless circles, and when he goes I'll go back to my place and you'll come with me.

"I want to go back to where the women are."

"You'll stay with me," the king said.

"But I'm afraid."

"And are you afraid of the king?"

"I'm afraid of the snake and the women carrying the animal and your eyes submerged in the whiteness. I'm afraid of your men who circle around you without you knowing."

"I do know, but I want, but I can't, but I . . . "

The stranger looked up and saw the bird descending. And he saw a beak descending. The man felt sharp knives ripping his clothes, he felt that his joints were snapping, he wept but I'm searching for my suitcase, I left papers in it and I don't want anything. And the bird descends and the man gets smaller and smaller, he became white like the white sand. He became like forests whose trees have been cut down, he became naked like the square and like the square he had no beginning. He tried to open his eyes and shout, he saw endless staircases, he tried to climb up, he went way up, he saw a hand stretching out to him, he grabbed onto the hand and climbed, his panting increased, it increased and stopped and then he fell to the ground.

The seventh woman said.

The first woman said.

And the blackness spread out and the hand stretched out to him. The women took him in their hands, they carried him and circled around with him. Then he found himself thrown onto the sand. He opened his eyes and saw the sand and the dust that surrounded his head and feet.

Woman, shouted the man. And his voice fell onto the ground of the square in circles, and they were the circles he had drawn on the sand with his finger slipping farther and farther away.

He looked at the distant voices, and he saw a dot coming near, and the dot was black and growing and he was waiting for it.

The woman calls to me, I say to her, I am not me.

I know you are not you, but she calls to me.

She calls me and I go, says the man as he listens to the rustling of her robe and sees the dust coming from under her bare feet and it pierces me all the way to my head.

IV

The Third Woman

This woman, said the man.

This man, said the woman.

And the voices were falling onto the white sand. The man stands and looks at a black face covered in black cloth and he tries.

This woman standing in front of me, the stranger said. And he wanted to look more, he wanted to tell her about the voices he heard at the grave.

This man standing in front of me, the woman said, and she wanted to ask him about the color of the king that he saw, but she didn't ask.

She approached him, she threw off her long black robe, she covered the man's head and walked with him and he walked. The stranger didn't see anything, he was like someone walking in colorless sand, and they were the colors that mingled in the square when he came to it for the first time, entering now into the robe of this woman who walks with him.

This is the third woman, the man said, he wanted to say, and all alone he walked, and the black robe covered everything.

The man opened his eyes, he opened them more, his

eyes widened to no end. I don't see, the man said. But she is the third woman. I want to remember. He shut his eyes in order to bring the memory back, he felt something burning in the white of his eye, he tried to put his hand on his mouth and licked it in order to get some moisture, he moved his right hand, it was something resembling an arm that moves while the hand is still. He moved the left, the arm was still and the hand wasn't moving. He couldn't say anything so he dozed off and didn't dream of anything. He dozed off like someone falling into sleep, or like someone fainting.

And after innumerable days, or the man can't remember them, he found himself in the middle of a long alley and in front of him walked a robe and around him were sticks planted in the middle of the alley, and everything was gray.

The man tried to sit on the gray ground, but the robe that was in front of him was moving and flying up into his eyes, so he walked behind it and he walked.

And amidst a silence enveloping his ears, the voices exploded. The man can't tell anyone how the voices began and they were like sudden thunderbolts. The woman looked back then she walked on. And the voices shake the houses, the clay reverts to walls stuck together, and numerous voices emerge from all directions.

And there is the stranger walking, the head bends forward a little, the body trembles and then bends down, and the voices pierce him from everywhere. Voices merge, voices of women and men and children and animals and birds and trees.

The woman looked back a third time. And the man saw something that resembles eyes. He saw blackness moving amidst water or what looks like water.

As though I'm in a well, the man shouted.

The woman's robe shook from behind and she began to run.

I was afraid, the man said, I am afraid. And he ran. And she was hurrying in the middle of a dirt road, and he hurried, and he panted, and he almost falls down, and he wants to go back to the square, and he wants to weep for the king.

But where is the king?

Where are you, your majesty the king?

Where . . . ?

And the man's voice began rolling in front of him like peels. And he saw what looked like a mountain that bows down before the bird. And he saw the woman coming back to him, she grabs him by the hands and takes him to another alley, and he smells the scent of the dirt that resembles the scent of winter, and she pulls him toward a narrow submerged door. She bends down, he bends down with her, she bends down farther until her head almost touches the dirt, he falls onto the dirt, she pulls him by his hands and he finds himself in a house with no windows.

An odor and a woman and a naked room.

The woman sits in the corner of the room and her panting increases, he stands in the middle of the room and he looks and tries to see. He felt something moving, he looked back and saw her. She was removing the scarf from her face, and her face was white and something was coming from it that resembled light diffracting on the walls of the room.

She bowed down and asked him.

But he doesn't know how to answer.

Where are we? he asked her.

This is a house, she answered.

"But why?"

"Because I want you to come with me."

"But how?"

She told him about the moon. The moon, she said, chooses a woman every three years, and permits her to come with a man to her house for a day and a night. And the moon has chosen me and you were there, so I took you in my robe and now we are in my house. Why don't you come closer?

"But who lives in this house?"

My children, the woman said, three girls.

"But I don't hear any movement."

"They are there, they'll come in a little while, but why don't you come closer?"

"I'm afraid" the man said. "I, I don't remember meeting you before now. What is your name?"

"Did I ask about your name?"

"No."

"Did I tell you about coming with me?"

"No."

"Did I, did I?"

"No, no."

"Come."

"No."

The woman came closer and sat beside him.

"But . . . "

"Don't ask, mister, enough."

"You're a virgin . . . "

"Yes."

"But how, where did the children come from?"

The woman lifted up her robe and said it was hot inside, and she said a lot of things. She told him that she wept a long time. I was young. And one of the women was buried next to the king, and I was new here, and I didn't know how I was supposed to weep, and I didn't want to go but my father, so I went and I didn't like to weep, but the women, so I wept. And I didn't like the long robe, but the robe, so I put it on. And I was weeping. I wept in a louder voice, and I was listening amidst the wailing to the voice of the woman who was whispering to me to weep less. And so I wept more. And I kept on weeping in a different voice, then the king called me over. The man who was guarding the tomb said the king wanted me. I went to him. I don't remember anything, there was blackness and there was something like a bird, but when I came out I was pregnant and I bore three daughters in three days. The man came and took the little girls and brought them to live in this house, and they will come in a little while.

And the stranger felt hungry, and he said he wanted to eat salt.

Salt, no, the third woman said.

She takes off her robe, she leans against the wall and stands naked. The shadows are gray and lean toward blue. I see the shadows, the man thought. And he looked at the body, the body was gray and leaning toward white, it was like a bow standing and bending down. The man began to feel something burning. The burning began in his stomach, then it extended higher, his face became full as if it would explode, then he felt his thighs and a warm pulse. He went toward her, he tried to say something, the voice shakes while the woman is in front of him. He took off his clothes, the clothes were sticking to his body as though they were his skin.

And when the man became naked he came closer to the woman, he stuck to her, he took her between his hands. His face comes close and she collapses onto the ground and he falls on the ground, and she comes close and produces sounds like she is crying. But she isn't crying, the man said, the sounds increase, the man comes close, he is upon her, he is in her, now he is standing at the high walls, now he is, but she is, what . . . but she is moving farther away, he saw her moving away then he heard the voices. Weeping increases, as though the whole house has transformed into voices. Voices of little girls and obscure words.

Get up. Get up, shouted the woman.

He got up. She put on her long robe, he put on what looked like a long robe, she sat, he sat.

"I am here," she shouted.

I am here, the echo answered.

She got up, then she came back. No one.

No one, the man said.

No one, the woman said.

She laughed and he laughed. She came close and he came close. She took off her clothes and he took off his clothes.

And here is this man with the woman, the square is far away and the weeping is far away. He took her hair in his hands, her hair flew about in the empty space, and the room grew wide, and he was.

The voices, she shouted.

I don't hear anything, he said.

The voices. Get up. And she shouted at the top of her lungs and got up. And there were the voices and three girls. And the woman said she was waiting for them, and she turned to him and said we'll try again. And she waited. I am here, she shouted, and the walls answered I am here.

But where are the children? the man asked.

My children, she said.

My children, he said.

Come, let's search in the other room.

"There are no other rooms in the house."

"Maybe out in the street."

"Impossible, we won't go out into the street."

The woman began to cry quietly. He sat beside her, he kissed her, he felt the taste of salt. Salt, no. Then she came close, and he came close a third time. She took him and he took her, they stuck together like two bodies stuck together in a locked room but . . . just when the woman was trying to whisper something to him, they heard footsteps and words. And everything was clear, and everything was waiting. He jumped to the door of the room: no one.

And the woman said no one. And she told him that they said she wouldn't sleep with the lonely man who waits in the square. They told me that the children will come and cry, but I didn't believe it.

We'll try again, the man said.

"You can't try anymore."

And the man tried again, and he discovered that things were no longer possible. The voices disappeared and the air surrounding him became heavy. The head hangs slightly forward, he sits or stands, he tries to speak.

The woman told him about a man who came a long time ago. He went with the woman to the end of the square, and there he asked for salt and he ate the salt. He would put it on his palm, rub his mouth with it, and swallow it. I don't know why, or why he wanted to eat salt. He ate salt and then asked for water. We got water for him and he drank. And the more he drank the thirstier he got, so he would drink, then he began to swell up. He transformed into a lump rolling in the middle of the square. His back arched, but he asked for the water and we would get him the water, and he didn't quench his thirst and he didn't eat. But he didn't die.

"Why didn't he die?"

I don't know, the woman answered. Maybe he died, maybe he didn't die, maybe the woman hid him inside her robe. Maybe.

"But why didn't he die? Take me to the square. I want to go back."

"But you didn't sleep with me, try again."

"I tried a lot, I want to go back to the square."

"But you're going to stay with me, and I'll take you to another place."

"I want the square."

I'll take you with me, you have to see the sea before you go back. We'll walk and we'll get there.

"But I don't want to walk, I want to roll on the sand again. I want to search for him so I can give him his clothes and go on my way."

"But you're going to come with me."

The sea is waiting for us, the woman said. And I want to see the blue sea swallowing me, I want to throw you there.

She held my hand, I held onto hers tightly, I was like someone climbing a high mountain, I was like someone trying to see. And here I am with her.

The stranger is with a woman whose name he doesn't know, and she tells him she is going to take him to the sea, and he waits, he told her he is waiting, he said to her and he bent down beside her and walked on a winding road full of broken pieces of wood.

V

This Sea

And I walked.

The stranger says he was walking, he says he walked and doesn't know more than that. The woman asks him while swimming in the water, he says to her that she's not in the water. She holds onto him, wet, smelling of a mixture of grass and dead fish.

But I don't see the dead fish, the man says. She comes close to him and gestures with her hand, he understands that he is supposed to jump, he understands that what is below is the sea she spoke to him about at length, when he asked her to be quiet and leave him to walk amidst that black darkness that resembled stacked clothes.

But he feels afraid and cold. I'm cold, he shouts, but he doesn't hear his voice, and the woman doesn't turn to look at him. She jumps and leaves him all alone. The man sits on a protruding rock and sees his long robe, which the woman put on him that night, and now the robe flies around him. He hears the sound of the fabric flapping in the wind coming from a place that resembles the gap in front of him that the woman called a sea.

This sea, he said in a loud voice, this sea doesn't look like anything.

He doesn't remember ever having seen a sea before, he remembers the white square in which the sand glimmers, and the white rock in which the robe glimmers, and the black robe that resembles the hides of skinned animals. But I don't see the animals, the man said. And once more she comes close to me, and once more he feels afraid.

She holds onto him with her wet hands and her robe, which falls down upon him and upon her.

"Come, let's jump."

"But the cold."

"The water is warm."

"But the salt."

"The salt dissolves in the water."

"But the fish."

"The fish are dead."

"But the light."

"I'll light things up for you when you jump with me."

She came closer, she dressed him in her robe. I am inside the water. Something resembling the color blue fell upon his eyes, and he was looking ahead and seeing. And the stranger didn't tell anyone about what he saw. He didn't tell and he walked. And again he saw himself amidst the blue color, which started to disappear. And the woman was around him, she raised her hand and pointed to the distance, and he couldn't see anything but the blackness that was spreading and spreading.

What is the color of the sea? the man asked.

This sea, she answered.

And her voice began to break up into small unintelligible sounds.

I can't hear you, the man shouted.

And the woman was answering with her words, and the man listened to the words but he didn't understand what they meant. He thought that the words resembled a story that a woman, who wore silvery clothes and glittered in front of one of the gates, had told him. But he doesn't remember the story now, or the woman didn't tell him the story.

I no longer remember. And he saw himself collapsing, flowing above an endless abyss. The limbs hide inside the robe, and the robe extends, and the man feels he is falling, and he doesn't bump into anything. He said to the woman when he saw her beside him, he discovered the woman when his hand touched something and he heard a voice, he said to her that he was in the sea. And the sea was sticky like oil and warm and the heat comes onto the body and the body becomes full of sweat mixed with this water. The man felt a force pushing him down, and his robe began to float up. He told the woman he wanted to scream, and she told him that she heard his voice. And a dim light began to flow from the cracks in the water. The light was down below and the man was being carried on the woman's hand, and he tried to float on the water and the light. And he saw. He said he could swim alone, he left her and saw the water. Something that looked dark green blended into the water and floated next to him, then the thorns began to pierce his body, and his skin began to swell. He stretched his hand out to his stomach and he held something that had no form, as though it were water or sand mixed with water, but it was slippery. He raised his hand, a slight pain began to descend from his stomach. He plunged into the water and tried to swim and change his direction. And what was stuck to his stomach followed him. He lifted his head and looked, and he saw that he had gotten very far away from the woman. He wiped the water stuck to his eyelashes with the palm of his hand and opened his eyes, and the fire began to come out from his eyes. The colors mix together and the eyes swell up and the thorns protrude from them and become implanted in the water and the stomach. He shouted. He heard the woman saying to him to come near. He tried to come near. Where are the rocks? He looked in all directions, he circled around in the middle of the water and the water got hotter and the body burned and the thorns sprouted from the eyes. The man circles around searching for the woman, and the woman is there but he doesn't see her. She goes toward him but he moves farther away. The man got very far away, he was swimming and trying to tear from his body whatever it was that was stuck to it. He moves farther away and tries to go back to the woman, then suddenly the woman became visible in the distance, swinging like hung clothes and the hand waves in the water. The man felt something like tears emerging from his body. He shuddered and began to tremble, it was joy. Certainly I'm trembling out of joy. I'll go back to her and ask her to take me to the house, and there I'll listen to the weeping of the little girls and wait.

The man started swimming toward her, the thorns come out of his body but he goes on, he tries to go quickly amidst this white foam that floats around him. I have to take off the robe, but he didn't take off the robe, he was afraid if he reached her and he was naked she would think that he no longer wanted her. The robe floats around him, and he floats. And in the distance she was there, it was as though she would appear and disappear, as though she'd transformed into two faraway people. He approaches, and the woman transforms into bodies standing at the end of the sea and beneath them are rocks and stones and a white color. He came closer to her and began to listen to what sounded like whispers. And the two people came closer and closer until they became one, then they divided into two all over again. And he heard her voice.

"Come, you'll see a beautiful animal. We're late, hurry up before I go."

The stranger stretched out his hand and four hands stretched out to him and pulled him out of the sticky water.

But I can't stand up.

And he heard a strange voice.

"Stand up."

It wasn't her voice, it was someone else's voice. And the other person was rising up next to the woman. He leans onto something white mixed with gray colors, he speaks and doesn't look at the stranger. But I saw the woman divide into two the man says. His skin appeared as though it was about to jump out of him. He scratched his stomach and tried to understand.

"Who's he?"

He looked at the woman, as he waited for the other man to disappear, so they could be alone together and return.

The other man leaned over the white thing, and the stranger saw a white knife shining, and the smell of dead fish, and the man spits and the woman is afraid.

"He is what?"

"You're asking about me."

"Yes."

"Ask me."

"I don't know you."

"But who are you?"

"It seems you've forgotten me."

"I've never seen you before."

"You've seen me."

The stranger thought, since he arrived in this city he hasn't seen but one old man sitting on a rock, nearly collapsing waiting for death. But as for this one no.

You no, the stranger said.

But I saw you, the other man answered. We, you don't know, we live in this city.

"And what do you do?"

"I fish, don't you see, these are my fish."

"But fish should be shaped like fish, this isn't a fish."

The woman laughed, the man laughed, as for the stranger, he felt the taste of salt and oil on his lips.

But where are all of you? asked the stranger.

The sea, answered the woman, they're fishing.

The other man had finished skinning the animal with many legs, and he began cutting it up into little pieces. He gave some to the woman and she ate. He gave some to the stranger and he took it between his fingers. It felt cold, the white piece slid and then fell onto the ground, the other man bent down and picked it up. He put it in his mouth and began to chew it.

Come.

The woman walked and took me along and we walked behind that man who was naked. Now, the stranger noticed that this man who fishes animals full of legs is naked, and he is wearing nothing but a small white cloth around his middle. And his shadow on the rocks was long, broken into pieces along the bends in the rocks.

"Where to?"

I don't know, the woman answered.

But she walked. And the road was long, stones and protruding rocks and something blue. And the other man walks above this blue thing that melts. The stranger tried to copy him, he lifted up his long robe and walked through this blue thing, and thorns began to sprout up on his body.

"Why do you leave me and go with him?"

The woman turned back, and she began to remove the blue thing melting on my body. And the blue thing was a head, like a head that shines, and it didn't have any eyes, its body was composed of six legs and it was melting the legs first then the head starts, as though it is sinking into dark holes, then it collapses and melts away.

"Are you afraid of it?"

"I'm afraid, it's dead."

"What is it?"

"It's called the lantern."

"But it doesn't give light."

"Lanterns don't give light."

The other man laughed, then where is the light from? It doesn't give light except when we take it to the shore. We leave it in the water to fill up on little fish that flee to it from the wild fish. We take it out of the water and it melts and turns into water.

"Are you afraid of it?"

"I'm afraid, but it's dead."

The fisherman sat and the woman sat beside him. He blew in my face. I moved away a little and I saw the lanterns climbing on my skin. I wasn't afraid. And it wasn't pain, it was something burrowing into my bones without pain.

The other man said I must jump into the water until they disappear. The woman nodded her head in agreement.

"Come with me."

"No. I'm going to stay with him."

"But you."

"But I'm with him."

The other man blew in my face, and I saw the blue animals transform into what looked like smoke. And the man was carrying the woman and raising her up, and around them was an animal with a huge body and eight legs.

The man takes his knife and cuts off the animal's limbs, he comes close to the woman, he bends down over her.

"But I'm afraid to go back in the water all alone."

The woman didn't turn around and she didn't answer. And the stranger walked, he turned and saw the woman plunge into her robe and the man plunged in next to her. And the stranger walked between the rocky protrusions, and his shadow was breaking apart, he sees the woman transform into two, and the two draw near and he gets farther away. Then he fell into the water. The water was hot and the blackness covered his face, and the taste of the white animal spread from his fingers to his mouth.

He said I'll go back and he doesn't know to where, he said I'll dive in and he doesn't know where, he said the woman, and he didn't look at her.

"Where's the man?"

She signaled with her hand that she was coming.

"Where's the man?"

She jumped into the water and was next to him. She took him into her robe.

"Where's the man?"

"I don't know."

"But you were with him!"

She plunged into the water, he plunged next to her, he held onto her. The body was and she was as if she were waiting for him, as if she were hot like the water. She wiped the thorns from his body and took him far away, she told him she'd take him back.

Why don't we escape? the stranger asked.

She didn't answer, and she plunged into the water. The stranger saw a light, the light was rising up over the horizon, he saw the sea and saw the woman's robe floating. He said I'll dive in after her. He dived in and didn't find anything under the robe.

The black robe floats on the water and the stranger tries to search and tries not to drown.

He searched a long time, and he didn't find.

He dived down, he carried the robe, shook it in the open space, and didn't find.

The stranger took the robe and swam toward the white rock. He got out of the water, and the black robe was heavy on his arm, and rocks cut his feet.

A stranger in front of this sea and a black robe and a lost woman.

And the man walked and walked, and he was searching for the house or the square. I'll go back to it, I'm alone in these rocks that break apart beneath my feet.

VI

And There Was Weeping

The city and the women and this night.

And the stranger was carrying the robe and walking along winding roads.

The women and this city. The man thought as he carried a wet robe he'd gathered from the sea. The robe was heavy, the robe and the water, the robe covers my face and my face is heavy as if it were other faces. The man remembered his suitcase and remembered he was carrying a mirror.

"I threw the mirror and I didn't find it."

And there was a long night and there was a man walking in a long night and walking, he didn't ask and he walked. The robe lay flat on the palms of his hands as if it were the body of the woman who disappeared. The odor hovered over the robe and the sea was heavy like oil and hot like an odor exuding from my body.

It's the smell of the sea.

Is this the sea and is . . . ?

The stranger said I'll return, he said and he returned, he returned and didn't find anyone, he found and he didn't remember and the robe fell onto his face. The man lay down on a stone wall between houses with no voices in them. The black robe is on top of him as he floats above water that comes out of the robe and wets his face and hair and beard. And the eyes were shut tight on a gray light and the body closes upon itself and the hand holds the robe.

Then they started to.

Everything was silent. But they started to come out of the robe and fill the city with their voices, stone animals, skeletons and a strange odor and a body filling up with bones. Pain did not exist. But the animals were the same animals, it was they, the ones he saw fleeing on the border of the square, no, the ones he saw circling around the king's coffin, no, the ones he didn't see, but when he sees them now and remembers he sees them as though he has seen them before, as if he was born with them, as though they were there since he first came, but now, now he feels as if they are his fingers covering his face or as if they are the eyelashes that shut the eyes.

He sleeps, and the great animals emerge with their little skeletons, they circle around him and circle around, they take him to faraway places, he goes with them and feels nothing but the taste of salt.

"Where are the men?"

"The city and the women, but I didn't see one man," the man said.

"The city is women, and the men are drowning in the sea."

The man remembered the voice of the old man he met in the city, his voice was like his hands. The man looked at his hands and saw the voice wrinkled and full of holes, he saw the purple veins encircling the hands, he bent down onto his hands, his lips came close to, he tried to and the taste of salt and of dead fish flowed out, and the fish were bloated with death and the great animals hovered around them and the man was.

The robe was heavy and the water was heavy.

The robe and the water, the city and the women. But the man was standing next to her, but the man was waiting for me, but the king . . .

The robe carried me far away. The man was lying on the stone wall and the robe was water and the hands were purple and the woman wasn't.

He said I lost her in the sea.

His body began to crackle, everything was turning into bones, and the animals full of the smell of the sea jumped onto the eyes and chest.

I'm dying, the man screamed.

"I'm dying far away and the woman isn't with me and I'm."

And the light of day didn't emerge from the seams of the robe, and day didn't come. And there was a long night and there was a man.

And after aeons the man didn't know where they came from, he found himself in the square, and there was the light and the white sand and the black dots hovering around the tomb and the tomb.

The man found himself drawing near, and he drew near.

He found himself among the women and there was weeping. The women sat on the ground, the heads bent down and the sand mixed with the robe that I carry in my hands while I'm in their midst.

The man asked.

The women came close to him.

He asked again.

He was wet with the robe, and the robe was sitting next to him without moving.

He asked about the city and about the women and about the king.

And the light was glowing on the sand of the square like silvery water covering everything.

The woman stood up. The heads rose up to her.

I will tell you, she said.

She backed off a little, she removed her black robe and shined in the whiteness that resembled the sand of the square.

"I shall tell."

She was white and her face was transparent.

The woman stood and said:

In the beginning they said the sea. I didn't know the sea. I was sitting in a low room and the sound of the sea echoed cold and my father was.

I said I would tell about the sea but I'm telling you about my father . . . My father wasn't bending down when he said let's go. He was standing in the middle of the room looking at me and had tears on his face. And my mother was standing next to him crying. And there were people I didn't know and there was an old man approaching. The old man took me by the hands and we walked. The roads were endless as we walked. And when we arrived at the sea my father was bending into two halves and dropping like white drops in front of me. But I walked. The old man said words I don't remember then he threw me into the sea and the ululation of the women increased. I didn't see the women. I saw my mother but I heard the ululations and felt like crying. He threw me and everything was black. The sea was night and I was alone. Then I felt that everything was shattering. The sea was glass and I was thrown in the middle of shattering black glass. And the glass changed into tiny pieces and the tiny pieces pierced through my body and the salt. The salt was in my eyes, the taste started to seep through the eye into the chest. And I was shattering into tiny pieces. Then they threw the robe and wrapped me in it. The hands tightened around the robe and on my pieces scattered among the glass, they wrapped me well and they tied me to a long rope and they walked. They were walking and I was listening to the sound of the rope as it penetrated the dirt and the wailing was faint.

And they arrived.

I heard them say they had brought me there, then they swung the rope and threw me to the king. And I didn't see the king, but I learned how to weep.

The woman was white, she spoke and she was white, like the white sand that filled the place, then the colors began to ooze out of the eyes. There were hands stretching out and black daggers and a woman changing into trembling red pieces in the middle of the square.

"And I."

I'm the one who doesn't know. I'm the one covered with the robe, I'm the one covered with the water, I.

The stranger said he would stand. He said he would draw near, and so he heard the voice of the last woman, she was standing by the daggers and screaming and her hand was a long, jagged stick with fire coming out of its tip. The man approached, and he saw the jagged stick before his eyes. He approached and the fire began to smolder in his insides, but he reached the trembling red pieces. He put his hand out and felt the strange animals with the tapered heads and he backed off. He backed off and the red pieces began to gather around themselves and wrap around the long black robe and draw close to the circle, and a faint weeping became audible, and the man saw the second woman.

This is not my city.

The woman stood up and said:

This is not my city. We were walking and we saw the walls and there was a man.

And the woman began to take off her black robe. And the body was covered with countless wounds, and the sores from which the yellow thing oozed spread and colored the breasts and the waist.

The man told me to wait. He said that the walls and this gate and he ordered me to wait by the gate, and when a stranger comes who doesn't know where or how, open the gate for him and go with him to the square, and there I will be waiting for you and you shall go to my palace and live until the end of time.

And so I waited.

I'm standing by the gate and I find no one. No one knocks and no one passes. Then I climbed to the top of the wall, perhaps I would see, and I saw. The dust was increasing and so I said he's here. The dust becomes denser and I see the horse the stranger is riding wrapped with dust and spears, then the dust unveils more dust and I see no one.

And the days give birth to days and the nights give birth to days and I'm up on high all by myself. And that man who said loomed in the distance with frightened eyes while I waited.

Then they started coming.

Flocks of pigeons started coming, they alighted on these two hands, they cooed with sadness and disappeared. I began to wait for them and they began to wait for me, and with the days, I started to gather some seeds for them,

I would put them on my palms and they would eat. Then all of a sudden I don't remember when but I remember that they began to grow in a strange way, they became strange birds and they would come and the blood started and these holes. I got scared, I came down from the wall and stood at the gate, they began to descend with their wings solid as brass and peck at my body. I cried and he came, it isn't he, it isn't the man who said he was waiting for me. Another man came and said it was he, he wasn't but I believed him, I didn't believe him but I followed him. He gave me a black rope and threw me in the middle of the square, and no one taught me how to weep, I saw the women and I wept and we wept.

The woman's body was slippery and it slithered on the sand. She got up and picked up the robe with her stick and gave it to the second woman, she put on her robe and went back to her place.

And I, I wasn't speaking, I see and I don't speak. I said I won't tell my story to anyone. I don't know the story, so what's there to tell?

"I know," she said and she got up.

The fourth woman got up and said:

I know. I know everyone's story, but I don't know my own story. I didn't see anything, actually I did see, I heard mumbling. Then a voice told me that the gate. The voice is still in my ears and I can still see the brass gate shining under a burning sun. But I don't know. I don't know. They brought me here or I came here or I forget. But I see the stick and I see the king. I weep because we all weep and I'm a virgin because we're all virgins and I die because we'll all die, but I don't know.

She circled around herself with her long robe and began to move away.

"But the robe, why don't you take off the robe?" the stranger asked.

And the woman circled, and around her ankles moist dust filled the place. Then the dust began to fly into the man's eyes, and he started seeing ghosts approaching and hands reaching out to his neck and robes taking refuge in his body.

I don't, he said.

And he heard her voice. Her voice was like water and he saw her floating. The robe floats, the man comes close to the robe and sees the women.

And he saw the fifth woman getting up.

"Listen, man."

The fifth woman stood up and said:

Listen, man, my father came. And my father was a servant in the palace. He would go to the king's palace and see nothing but graves. And my father used to clean graves and plant flowers and the city was filled with flowers, and my father never saw the king. He knew that the king was satisfied with his work. An old woman who worked inside the palace used to tell him. And so he would come home filled up, he would sing and pick me up and fly away with me. Then he said marriage. And he said a man would come and take me far away. He sat me down in front of him and my mother was there and there were people staring at my face, and he spoke to me about obedience. I bowed my head obediently, and I waited. But he didn't come. He didn't come. My father said words to my mother and my mother said we must wait. And we waited. Then a stranger came and he was asking about the gates, I thought it was he, he took me with him and I found myself here, and here I am. We walked together and then he disappeared in the middle of the square, and in the middle of the square I saw the women. And the woman who carries the stick in her hand came, she ripped off my clothes, threw me to the ground, and dressed me in a black robe.

And now I'm in the circle.

"And you are he."

She looked at the stranger and said:

"How could you forget, you're the man."

"I, I don't remember, I don't. I'm looking for my mirror that got lost and for my things that I lost."

He said to her he wasn't the one and she was mistaken.

She approached him, he stood up, she opened her mouth and blew in his face, and the stranger's hair started tinging with white and the wailing rose up high.

The man sat and wept, and when his tears reached his lips he remembered the taste of salt and he remembered the eyes that had mesmerized him on the walls.

The odor rose and the sixth woman got up. And there was dust.

The sixth woman stood up and said:

I don't.

She said as the dust surrounded her.

I'm the one who from the beginning. I've been here from the beginning, my mother said and everyone said and I say. I'm where I've been from the beginning with the king next to me and I weep.

She backed off and her robe began to tremble amidst a wind that surrounded her, and there was fire and lights and a distant wind. And she was receding.

Don't let her, the woman carrying the stick shouted. Don't let her go, grab her, she is vanishing, hold onto her robe, it's flying.

The man got up and fell down.

I go.

"You stay in your place."

The man stayed in his place and heard voices and saw ropes and bodies being dragged by the ropes, and he saw his head tied to a white rock, then he heard her voice and saw the stick in her hand.

She was standing and she was calm. She uncovered her face and so the man saw the branches and the dry leaves dropping onto the feet.

She was in the center, she threw the stick and blew, and out came smoke and water. Then the tip of the stick began to move, and the red serpent started to jump, it reached the woman and so the wind quieted and went back. The snake turned back, then it jumped and went away. The women screamed, the city screamed, and the serpent ran far away, the woman followed it and then asked:

"Where is the third woman?"

One of the women came close to him and said in a hoarse voice:

"If the serpent flees, the city will die. And if the city dies the king's grave will be destroyed, and if the king's grave is destroyed everything will end."

There were voices and there was the stranger asking:

"But how?"

"The third woman," they answered. "Only the third woman knows how to catch the serpent. She went with you."

He said she went with him but she disappeared in the sea.

"But how?"

"I left her and came back, and this is her robe."

And the robe was heavy.

The man ran and the water was drenching the ground.

"I can't."

"Run."

He ran and threw the robe onto the serpent. Everything calms down, everything stops, everything is in its place.

"The stick came back," the woman said.

She raised the robe and pulled the stick and returned.

And suddenly the voices started. The stone animals emerged from inside the robe and jumped on the women, the women tried to get away and the small animals clung to the robes and their voices started to muffle among the bodies.

The first woman said we flee.

The second said we can't.

The fourth said we jump to the king.

The fifth said no, the grave should not be tainted.

The sixth said we die.

The stick said I don't know.

And the stranger saw black robes approaching one another and disappearing into one another, and he saw holes in the robes and he saw.

And there was weeping.

And the stranger wept.

VII

The Storyteller Said

The storyteller said that it faded away. The city that faded away.

The storyteller said:

And the story doesn't end here, because stories don't end this way, women running in every direction and a stranger who doesn't know, and small white rocks in the shape of small animals buzzing in the ears and white dust spreading on the square and a city whose name we don't know but we tell its story that doesn't end.

The storyteller said:

The little white animals came out jumping in the air. And they were innumerable, they jumped as though they would fly and then fall to the ground and jump again. The woman carried the stick and started to wave it in the air, the dust rose up and the women around her ran among the little animals and the stranger backs away and doesn't understand, he asks and doesn't get an answer.

The women gathered in a corner near the stones of the grave, and there was weeping. Then the weeping waned to faint moaning and the stranger weeps and tries to come near, but he feels as though the sand is eating him. He feels something like drowning.

"I can't move forward."

The man shouted then his voice began to disappear very slowly, and the words in his mouth became filled with a sour taste.

The stranger saw.

He saw the city drowning in the whiteness and he saw the white eyes widening and growing and he saw the women leaving for faraway places.

There was light, and the man was unable to come closer. And the light was little animals, bones hovering around the black robes and eating them, small eyes that have an odor.

He heard the women's voices. It's the first time he listens to the voices and remembers.

And the weeping women were in front of the corner of the grave talking about the odor. He sat in the middle of the sand and he heard, there was buzzing and there were the women. The women's voices and a strange buzzing sound droning everywhere. And the voices had the odor of voices.

The stranger said that he sees small white teeth. The teeth are locked shut and the words come out.

One woman said it isn't like the odor of the sea.

Another woman said it's the odor of the king.

This one said and that one said.

The woman who carried the stick stood up and spoke about the prophecy and said:

The king died. And before the king died he sat on his throne and summoned his ministers and said:

This white city resembles graves. And when, after my death, a strange bird comes and circles seven times above the grave, know that a deadly disease will spread in the city and kill everyone. And when everyone dies a king will come from far-off lands and travel by sea and destroy the walls. He is the king whom I do not know but for whom I waited, and here I am, dying, and he won't come until after my death.

"But he didn't speak about the strange odor."

"But he didn't weep."

"But he didn't see the man."

"But he didn't know, because he doesn't know, because he died."

The man heard and wept.

And the women faded away. The woman carries the staff, all the women carry staffs, the buzzing of the little animals and black robes thrown onto the sand and the women fade away.

The stranger felt sadness but he didn't know what was causing it.

"They're fleeing from the square. Who will mourn for the king after today and who . . . "

The man tried to move forward. And he discovered the sand was swallowing him up and he wasn't moving forward. Then he discovered he was walking on his hands and knees, he looks high up and sees the grave fade away. He is panting, the panting increases, he moves forward and the women fade away. White bodies full of screaming but they fade away and I try. The man tried a lot.

The storyteller said that the man was trying to pick up the little animals, and that he felt afraid. The women leave him alone and he doesn't know anything.

The man's sorrows grew and his fears increased. Then everything disappeared.

The man got tired of running and he sat, he saw and he didn't see the women, he saw the black robes as though they were discarded corpses, and he saw the white insects jumping on top of them, but he didn't see the women.

And the man sat all alone, and alone he said he would go on. He said I'll go back. He said everything had come to an end. He said it was he but he forgot how: the third woman, the woman who disappeared in the sea, the woman who was kidnapped by a tall dirty man who took her with him, she's the one, the one who ruined everything.

But I'm all alone. I speak and no one listens to me. I speak and I fear. I'm afraid and hungry and I want to.

The man lay down all alone in the square and the little animals came close to him, their odor permeated his eyes and his nose: they'll eat me and I'll die. The man thought that the women, when they come and look at his bones the voice of one of them will rise up saying he is the king. I won't become a king until I die. I won't become a king until the foul-smelling animals eat me . . . The man smiled or his lips moved as if he were smiling or wincing in pain. He shut his eyes and went to sleep, and the little animals slept around him and the voices slept, and the city began to fade away.

The storyteller said:

And it was told that the man slept a long time. He would try to get up, he would open one eye and not see and think he was still asleep. And the stone animals became fond of the man, they would hover around him and walk on top of his discarded body, then little by little the animals began to relinquish their hostility and they found in the man's body a place to sleep. They sleep and he doesn't see, he feels as though his body has become heavy but he doesn't see. He sleeps and sleeps as though he's never awakened, as though he wasn't the stranger that was, as though he hadn't seen the women and hadn't asked the gates and hadn't wept.

The storyteller said:

And the man got up, once the man got up just like that, he shook the piles of sand and the insects from his body and got up.

He saw that the city was gray, everything was gray. He stood up and circled around the grave. He was circling and moaning faintly, bowing his head down and circling around the grave. And he circled seven times then he backed away.

It's the tree.

He saw a black tree with a black trunk and black branches.

Where did the tree come from?

The man asked. Is it possible that? Is it possible? And he asked a second time.

He went toward the tree, and he said that he can now. Now I can sit in the shade of the tree. And he remembered trees and green grass, he remembered rivers flowing in valleys full of green reeds that reach up, he remembered cities he had seen and he remembered the women.

"But the women."

He got up. The man decided to go to the streets and alleys. To go to the old man who looks like the forefathers and ask him about the secret of the women and the secret of the grave and the secret of the king. But he was tired, he said I'll go later, and he sat beneath the tree and the little animals started coming near. The square is now filled with the animals, heads that move and skinny little bodies. The animals come to him, he smells their odor and he gets used to it, and the man felt hunger tearing him apart. And he saw the animals that swarmed around him, and he saw what looked like food. And he wasn't afraid, he grabbed a handful of the little animals, he brought his mouth down onto them and started to eat. Some of them went in between his teeth and some of them jumped onto his lips, and he eats. The sounds of the bones cracking between his teeth and the smell of blood. But he was eating and feeling more hunger. The man holds his hand out on the ground and the animals come with bowed heads, jump onto the hand surrendering and he eats and they crack under his teeth, and the blood spreads on the lips and the smell of blood and a strange taste that resembles the sea.

And when the man was full he walked around the black tree that grew on the edge of the grave and started circling around it.

The man circles around and the tree bends down over him as if it is covering him.

"I won't go," the man said. "I can't go, how can I leave the grave and these little animals and this sleeping king?"

And the man decided to stay.

He would circle around the grave then circle around the tree then go to sleep. And there wasn't light.

The storyteller said:

The lit-up square became dark, and the stranger became alone in a dark square, he didn't hear anything but his own voice and didn't see anything but his animals and he weeps. Then the weeping began to trail off and die out. He weeps softly and sleeps and doesn't think about anything but that he can't leave the place.

The storyteller said:

And things started to change, the light began to slowly turn to darkness and the distant voices began to come from the city and penetrate the square. And the man decided to go and see. He left his little animals and the grave and he walked toward the city. The man was afraid of getting lost, but he walked. And after countless days the man reached the dirt alleys that give off the smell of blood. He walked between the alleys and among trees with broken branches, and the man met a man sitting in front of a demolished house. The stranger asked him, and so he pointed with his finger and said there.

"But I don't know how to get there."

The man cleared his throat and pointed with his finger, there.

"I don't know."

"You don't know."

"No."

"How."

"I'm a stranger."

It appeared as though the man didn't believe that but he walked beside him and led him to a narrow place and left him all alone and returned.

And there he saw.

The storyteller said that the man saw everything. He saw the bodies stacked up on top of one another, he saw the sea with its black color and its black waves, he saw the women weeping over bloated corpses reeking of death.

"But what?"

"It's the epidemic."

"From where, the cause?"

"I don't know."

"What will you do?"

"We'll leave the city."

"Where to?"

"We don't know."

"How can you go and leave the grave?"

"I don't know. No."

"Will you stay?"

"And you?"

"And I."

"And I."

"And they and we and . . . "

We'll all stay, answered an old woman whom the man hadn't seen before. She was bending over dry leaves and chewing something.

Then he saw.

The storyteller said that the stranger saw bodies running in every direction and voices rising up. He sat next to a group of men who were eating something placed in front of them on the ground. He ate with them and told them about the grave. He said that the women fled and left him all alone. He said impossible. He said I'll go and search in the sea. He said the sea.

But they are there, everyone is there and the women too and they'll come back.

I'll go and wait, the man said. I'll go and clean the grave and put the little animals in their places and.

"But you're tired."

The stranger said his back was breaking from so much bending, but I'll bend down. I can't.

And he went.

"But wait . . . "

And he saw the third woman, she was wearing her black robe and leaning on a long staff and bending down.

"I'll go with you," she said.

"I won't go to the sea," he answered her.

"Let's go to the square."

"But you."

She laughed. I was afraid, she said. I smelled the odor between your teeth and I knew, but I'm going to return, we'll all return to the square, and you?

The stranger walked next to her and didn't speak. He saw the people bending down over the dirt of the alleys and he saw the city get smaller and enter into the night and the man returned to the square.

The storyteller said:

The city had never known anything like this. Babies died when they smelled the odor of the sea, and the people were perplexed, how do we keep back the sea, how can the odor be stopped . . . They were burying their children in little graves and asking. Then they saw the women coming. The women without robes running toward the sea. The women sat alone and no one dared to come near.

The woman carrying the stick said and walked alone in the streets asking about a woman who got lost in the sea and she told about a man weeping in front of the grave and about stone animals that get inside one's clothes.

And no one believed her.

They said she was afraid.

And they said she fled from the square and she must go back.

And the woman was trying to say that the square was full of dust. But she went back. They all went back.

The storyteller said:

And the stranger was sitting all alone. The voices no longer were the same voices. He sits in the square and waits and doesn't look at the women. He listens to the faint weeping and doesn't feel at all curious, but he stays. He doesn't move from his place the whole day long. But the people living in the alley believe that they used to see a man with a hunched back walking at night along their alley.

He would go in the direction of the sea and not speak to anyone.

The storyteller said:

The city had never known anything like this. And after the return of the women, the people living in the city started hearing a strange howling sound coming from the direction of the square. Some said it came from these animals that had become part of the square, and some didn't say anything, they would open their lips and not speak.

And the stranger didn't speak. He said at one time he would wait and he stayed in his place and the voices surrounded him.

The storyteller said that it faded away.

The city faded away and the voices became submerged in endless turns and bends.

And the man was far away, in the square far away, bending down onto himself as though he was a circle moaning faintly.

VIII

The Stranger

And I say, I am the one who says, I am the one who.

But I no longer remember, and this square doesn't remember, and I am here. My back bends over an odorless ground, and I see the whiteness. This whiteness that plunges into my eyes, this whiteness and this square. I see and I see the women.

And the stranger was there. He says to the women and the women are around him listening to him. Their bodies undulate inside long black robes and they listen. Bodies and a hesitant voice and whiteness in the eyes.

The man for countless years, and the odor exudes from the hands, as if the hands had become mine, as if I am the hands, the stranger says, as if I am the square.

The man said words and the man heard voices and he remained where he was and didn't think.

He said that he is here. And the women were all around him and next to him asking and he answers.

And the square is big and white, the white square and I am here.

And the man saw.

He saw that things had a new taste to them. The sand

and the stone animals and the women. Everything changed, even the weeping was different.

She said to him that the weeping is rising up from the city. And the man saw fire on the outskirts of the city and listened to intermittent wailing filling the skies, and he looked and there were the women. Everything was looking over there, even the coffin, the woman carrying the stick said to him that the coffin stands up and walks at night. And that she saw him, she saw the king, the king who has been sleeping for endless years gets up at night and walks along the dirt roads, and he cries with the wailing that rises up from the sea.

And she told him unbelievable things, she said that everyone, that the dead were everyone, and that this thing killing the children we know no reason for, this thing that kills will kill everyone.

And the man thought he wanted to die. He thought he was dying. He said I want to die. And she told him to wait. She said that the women stopped weeping, and that she no longer knew, and that no one comes to the grave, no one visits the grave where one must come, and the grave comes.

The storyteller said:

That things are just what they are, things, and this happened a thousand years ago and will happen again in a thousand years. And the storyteller was laughing, laughing in a loud voice so that his face was engraved like fallen branches, but he was laughing. And he said that the women.

And the first woman said, the woman carrying the stick said that the women and that the city and that the king and that the stranger. She said that they don't know, but I don't know. This hasn't happened before, it hasn't happened that everyone and I have not remained except alone.

And the stranger saw, he saw himself alone and the women going. This time I will not go and bring them back here, I will leave this city.

The stranger said he would leave. He said I'll pack my suitcase. But he remembers, now he remembers, the suitcase is torn in the sand and the letters are lost and the walls, I don't know where their gates are, and the sea is full of black robes.

And he sat all alone.

And the city was the city.

A city with no gates, and the voices emanate from its inner alleyways, and the alleys are full of women and men coming out of clay houses and leaving. And the crowds of people became more numerous. Some go to the sea and don't come back, and some go to a faraway place and walk along barren soil filled with brackish waters.

And the women were leaving. And the voices that filled the square depart for nowhere. And the man sits all alone, he knows and he tries.

He said I'll try. He said I want to go, I won't stay in the square and I won't.

The man got up, he leaned onto the shoulder of a lonely woman who stayed by his side.

Everyone left me, she said. I wanted, I want to stay. Why don't you stay with me?

He said to her let's go and see.

There's no point in going, she answered. I saw everything. I have to stay and you have to stay next to me. We won't find another place where we can cry over a grave, and we won't find another city, and I won't find another man.

She stood next to him. Her voice was light and soft. She resembled mothers, the man thought. And suddenly he felt his body trembling with weeping, and he remembered a hand and a forehead, he remembered a face covering his body and a voice calling him by names he has forgotten.

He took the woman's hand and they sat down, and they were alone in the middle of a square filled with many voices, and they were weeping silently and calmly.

She said, "Why?"

I don't know, the man answered.

She fell silent and he fell silent.

She looked at him and asked him why he didn't sleep with her that night. She spoke about a moonlit night and about trees and knee-high grass. She spoke about a past love and about a dream. She told him she would leave the square with him.

Do you know, she said, if you had accepted we would've gone far and lived in a little house on the seashore. But you refused and your eyes were clouded and you were thinking about something I don't know what it was.

The man said he doesn't remember that she asked those things of him. I came and there were the women and I hadn't heard these words before. I was looking for her and you weren't with them. I don't remember you, the man said.

The woman spoke a lot and said that she waited. I waited for you, she said. I was sure you would come. And you came alone, what would a lonely man do in the middle of a square filled with weeping, he would come to me and I would take him and we would go. But you didn't come. If you had come, if only you had come, we would have lived there and our children would've filled the sea, and we would have gone out of the square and lived as others do. But you were I don't know what, I didn't understand I tried you I don't know what, I don't understand what you were doing and why.

The man bowed his head and said he was ready to go with her to the city.

Now, she answered, now that everything has come to an end we can no longer do anything.

It would have ended in any case, the man answered. The children would've died as all the children are dying now, and we would've been alone just as we are now.

The man said that he doesn't believe the story, but let's suppose it's true, and that I accepted and we went, what would be different? We would've sat in front of the sea and waited, we would've come to the grave and waited, we would've given birth to the children and waited, then the children would die and we would die.

And he laughed. He got up and she got up, he leaned on her shoulder and they walked together, they reached the clay houses, the odor of the city emerged as it filled up with the corpses the people were burying, and they heard the sound of the sea as it crashed against the thorns.

They sat alone on a mound of soil and the crowds of people who passed by swelled and they were passing by, women with black robes and men with bowed-down faces, the woman sitting beside the man asks where to and the people don't answer.

"Where to?"

She said to there. And she pointed with her hand to the distance.

"And for whom shall we leave the city?"

The city, nobody, said the man.

And in the distance his features began to appear. He was a young man and he was small, carrying on his back a swollen leather suitcase, looking right and left, and asking and no one answers, he moves forward and doesn't know where to. His eyes wandering he looks at the distance and he doesn't see.

It's as if he doesn't see the stranger sitting next to the woman said.

He doesn't see, the woman said.

The man approached and stood before them. He hesitated a little and then asked about the square. He approached the stranger sitting next to the woman and looked at him with perplexed eyes.

"But you, but you are sitting with a woman, you were supposed to be alone, she told me, I met her in front of the wall and she told me that you were alone, that you'd show me the way."

And he told his story.

And they were listening to him and his voice was trembling.

"But you," the stranger interrupted him.

"But I knew that the disease . . . while I was coming to look for you, maybe we can run away from here, maybe."

"You came too late," the stranger answered. He told him that that was no longer possible now.

He said he wanted to take him. I'm searching for a child that got lost here, the man said, and this child was coming from a faraway place, and I'm prepared for anything.

"You're not prepared for anything," the stranger said. "Everything has passed."

The woman said let's get out of here, and he said he'd come with us. I said no, I told him to go back to where he came from.

"I can't," he answered, "I don't know how."

"Go with them," I said to him.

"They don't know me, they don't speak and they don't answer. They sit like this or walk like this. I saw them circling around the walls like the blind, I asked them about you they don't answer and I didn't understand anything. I understood from the screams of a woman that she was talking about the fire, where's the fire, I don't see the fire."

And we were sitting, he sat down next to us.

I told him he should have come before now. Before now I could've helped you, the stranger said.

And the dialogue is between the two men, and the woman looks at the ground and sighs.

"Come, let's go," she said.

The woman stood up:

"Come, let's go to where the sea is."

The sea, no, the stranger answered her.

I'll go with you, said the other man. Maybe we'll find something there.

And they went.

And the stranger remained all alone, looking at the faces of the passersby, seeing the crowds of passersby as they run away from the city to an unknown place that they don't know.

He stood up and asked.

He asked a man and he asked a woman and he asked everyone and didn't listen to an answer, he put his head between his palms and went to look for the woman and for the one who came late.

If he had come before now, the stranger thought, if he'd come he would've found the women standing in front of their palaces and he would've entered places he couldn't even dream of, if he'd come before now. But he's here and I can't. I tried to tell them that we shouldn't cry, we must find the gates. But . . . the truth is I didn't say anything, I wanted to say, but . . . no now I want to say, now after everything has happened I think that I wanted to say, or that I should've said. Now, I want to be there in order to say. But I'm not there, and I don't say anything.

And the stranger walked and walked. He walked innumerable days and he walked. And the roads gave birth to roads and the dust gave birth to dust, and he walked. The streets led to other streets and the alleys ended in other alleys, and he walked.

And he was walking and asking about a woman who went with a man to the sea, and the smoke spread. He saw a man sitting on the side of the road, he asked him, and the man who was sitting on the side of the road was all alone, bending down and putting his head between his hands and the white hair covering his head and his hands. He approached him and asked him. The man raised his head up and pointed to the distance.

"Everyone is there, don't you see the smoke, it's the fire, everything is burning."

He left him and went on, but the man stood up and walked beside him, and they walked together. He spoke words the stranger remembers he had heard before, as though they came from a distant place in his memory.

"But you."

"But I."

"No, I don't know you."

"And I don't know you."

"But, what is happening."

"I don't know, and you?"

"I'm asking."

He left him and walked, and was looking where the smoke was, then the fire began to spread. And the fire was crawling between the houses and the gates and the faces.

The fire was blue and yellow and the colors glowed in the eyes.

The stranger said he was dying all alone. He said and he looked and he saw the fire devouring everyone, he caught a glimpse of the woman and the man, he caught a glimpse of the women, and they were all being colored by this light blue that spread over the eyes.

He said he is dying, and he heard the screams of death. The people were screaming. Then the screaming died out for a moment before it started again.

He looked and saw his clothes burning with these colors, and he saw himself sinking farther and farther. And he saw, he was in the square and the square was on fire, and he saw, he was in the alleys and the alleys were on fire, and he saw, he was in front of the walls and the walls were on fire. Everything, the women and the coffin and the grave and the houses, everything, even the sea, the sea was colored with blue. This is the color of fire, this is fire, this is I but I don't hear the voices now. This is I.

The stranger moved forward, and the people were forests on fire, approaching one another and collapsing. And the odor was the same, the odor of the square where the king is, the odor of old embers extinguished with water, and the brackish water was on top of him and around him.

The storyteller said.

Then the sea came. The sea ate up the fire and spread over the city. The sea ate up the walls and spread over the gates, and the gates collapsed, and the remains of corpses floated over a blue rooftop and dark domes. Everything was floating, and nothing remained of the city except weeping voices coming from the entrails of the fish and rising to where no one can listen to them.

Elias Khoury is a lecturer at the American University in Beirut and has also taught at Columbia University. He is the literary editor of *al-Nahar* newspaper and has published book-length works in various genres, including novels, critical essays, and short stories. His novels include *Little Mountain,* which was published in English translation by the University of Minnesota Press in 1989, and *The Travels of Little Gandhi,* published in Beirut in 1989 and forthcoming in English translation from Minnesota.

Paula Haydar is a free-lance translator living in Amherst, Massachusetts.

Sabah Ghandour teaches in the Department of Oriental Studies at the University of Pennsylvania.